The

WELL

of the

NORTH WIND

A NOVEL

KENNETH STEVEN

Marylebone House

First published in Great Britain in 2016

Marylebone House
36 Causton Street
London SW1P 4ST
www.marylebonehousebooks.co.uk

British Library Cataloguing-in-Publication Data
A catalogue record for this book is available from the British Library

ISBN 978–1–910674–25–3
eBook ISBN 978–1–910674–26–0

Typeset by Graphicraft Limited, Hong Kong
First printed in Great Britain by Ashford Colour Press
Subsequently digitally printed in Great Britain

eBook by Graphicraft Limited, Hong Kong

Produced on paper from sustainable forests

For Barbara McDougall of Lismore

The boy liked to draw in the sand. He liked to take his finger and drag it in whorls and arcs so a dark pattern was left behind. He crouched above the grey sand that shone with the memory of water. He was five summers old now and whenever his mother did not need him this was where he came. It was a beach held between the claws of the rocks; he had learned the little path that snaked down from the upper ground – it was a place protected on all sides by rocks. Well, on three sides – the fourth was open to the sea, the blue-green play of water in constant shift with light and shadow. Sometimes, when his forefinger was sore with drawing, he sat on a red rock with his feet tucked up close under him, to watch the sea come in about him. But that was only on days when the sea was soft; at other times he stood on the shore as the waves drove in, the sky beyond a slate-grey, serpents clustering in the whites of the waves, breaking on the shore in a bright silver. Then he felt small; he hid his hands from the cold and he felt smaller than his brothers and sister – strange and a little frightened. He was excited and frightened at one and the same time, and he did not know what to do.

But this was his place nonetheless, and he did not want his brothers to find it. The beach was in his mind all the time; it lay at anchor in his consciousness and he went to it in his imagination when he could not go there in reality. For there was fresh water to bring from the well, there was the fire to tend, there was his sister to comfort, there were sticks to bring . . .

It was a long time since his father had not come home. He had gone for birds' eggs on the stack with two of the other men because they were so hungry in winter. A child had died and storm had rattled the headland for endless days. So his father had gone but had not come back. The two other men returned with eggs but they were silent, their eyes scattered and strange. One of them had bent to him and taken a soft finger over his cheek and looked away. He had gone to his mother but his mother had not wanted him; she had bundled him away and hidden in the darkness of the earth house. He had felt her shaking. He had wandered with hunger and he had not known the place he came to, but someone held him and put something that tasted sweet and slippery in his mouth. He had fallen asleep warm and wakened to skies torn between blue and grey. He was frightened to go back home and he hovered outside, a salt stinging in his eyes – but suddenly his mother saw him and ran to him and held him.

That was a long time ago. He only remembered fragments of his father now; they were like the tiny pieces of kindling he found between rocks, the dry sprigs that were best for lighting fires. He remembered him singing early in the morning; he remembered the colour of his eyes; he remembered the shape of his back. But he could not remember his voice. He went searching through the caves of his head in search of his father's voice, but he could not find it. He cried at night for it and could not understand where it had gone. He wanted to tell his mother but instead he just huddled in to her, right in to the darkness of her and the smell of her skin, and cried.

*

2

One morning he was drawing in the sand. He had not been allowed to go to the beach so he had run there all the same; he had shouted defiant words to his mother that were caught like twigs in the wind and blown away. He had come down to the beach and crouched there as always, but he felt a knot somewhere inside him that would not go away. He felt it when he swallowed. There was a pool of water in front of him, a pool that ruffled when the wind came, that was driven from a still mirror to a grey flickering. But suddenly he saw it had grown dark with shadow, with a brown shape. He looked up into the face of a man.

He did not think to be angry, though this was his place and he had not wanted to share it, not with anyone. There was no time to think of anger; he was just taken aback, amazed. The man had a wide face and small, bright eyes that glittered. The skin of his face was very white; it was drawn tight over its frame.

'What is your name?'

The voice was kind, not like the voice of the man who shouted sometimes for him to go and get water or tend the fire. That voice hurt the inside of the heart; it made the soles of the boy's feet somehow feel raw. This voice was gentle, and though it was not his father's, it made him think of the ghost of his father's voice, the voice he had searched for and lost a long time ago.

'Fian.'

'How would you like to learn to write, Fian?'

The boy did not understand the question. A breeze came over the beach and ruffled the dark hair over the forehead of the man with the white face. He looked down and saw the things he had drawn in the sand, the shapes and pictures. He looked out to sea as a white edge of water broke over rocks. Then the man leaned forwards and took his right hand softly in his own; he extended the forefinger, brought it down to the sand and made it draw one long straight line. Then at the top he made the boy's finger curl a circle. He brought another line down beside the first, but this one went longer and then came backwards, curling at the end also. Then hidden in one of the curls he made Fian's finger draw a face; a forehead and a face and a beard. Then he let Fian's finger go.

'How would you like to learn to write?' he asked again, and now his voice was even softer than before. Fian looked up and he thought of his father again, though he did not know why. He heard the patter of his heart under his woollen cloak and he nodded.

*

The monks had chosen that place because of the water: not one well, but seven. There in that gnarled place of limestone; that old porous bone of a headland with its caves and its crumbling. They had come there and the people thought them strange, but not strange enough to drive them out. Strange enough to ignore; strange enough to leave alone. Their chapel was at the very edge of the land, at the land's end – a place that no one in all their madness might want. The wind blew there from all the corners of the world, and the bare pavement of limestone was treeless, bush-less, useless. The people called it the place of ghosts; there were stories of white

4

horses, of sea creatures, of white beings from the sky. It was a place where time was torn, but it was no good place. For that reason they did not grudge the monks their chapel, their bare dwellings – they thought them mad and left them to their madness.

But the water was sweet. There, in the middle of that giants' chessboard of wrecked slabs of stone, a fist of pure, good water sang upwards, glistening. It was as though it had waited for them, known of their coming. It was a gift. But the monks had other water too: they had the sea. They understood wood and they knew the waves; they shaped boats and they learned every cave and headland, brought home spillings of silver fish and gave names to the skerries, the whirlpools, the beaches.

They had brought with them one fire, one cradled handful of fire that must never go out. It was set among the stones of the chapel, and though it was torn this way and that in the winds, it never went out. It flickered beside the cross of quartz. One spring, word came to them that the people of the settlement had lost their fire. Ten days there had been storm and the coast was bruised and dazed; at last the sea breathed in and out, and light seeped from a low sky. They wasted no time; the moment they heard they began carrying light, sheltering it and watching it until it had been delivered. It was brought into the earth house without a word. The sore, white faces had looked up, wondering and dumb. It had been Marua who had thought of the gift.

*

And in the springtime that followed, Marua went back to them, to the people to whom he had brought light and fire. The blue sky

5

broke above, and in the limestone land pink and yellow sprigs grew and fluttered in the breeze. There were birds, tiny nothings of things that came in waves through the spring air. Marua came back to the people and he crouched in the earth house, the same place to which he had carried the fire, and he told them about the light that had come to earth. He told wonderful stories of the light and they listened, amazed and silent. He visited the earth house when the moon had floated up from below the sea and the stars crystalled the night sky, for then his path was clear along the limestone tableland. Then, too, the men had come back from their edges of field; the children slept and they had time to listen. They said nothing, but the story of the light stayed with them; they carried fragments of Marua's words and could not forget them. And one day three of the men came like shy, unbroken horses to the chapel out at the place of ghosts; they waited until Marua had come to them and then nodded, and he brought them to the spring and put a hand of water over their foreheads, and one of them cried.

All that had been many years before, but it was how the bridge was built. There was a path now between the earth houses and the chapel. So that morning when Fian saw the brown shadow in the pool of brine and looked up into the strange, wide face – he knew at once where the man came from. Marua himself was old and wandered and grey; his days of carrying the light were done, but his eyes were no less generous. The young monk who found Fian was called Innis; he was only two years gone from his own family and he missed his little brother.

*

6

At first Fian did not talk about Innis. So much of his world was shared: the place where he laid his head, the place where he ate and went to wash, the place where he dressed. When he buried his head in the soft place close under his mother's arm it was likely a younger brother had done the same on the other side. On the day he first met Innis he came home and had a burning hand to remind him of the words he had spoken when he left. He went to bed in a curled ball, his cheeks salty and angry and defiant. Innis was his. He did not understand what he wanted to give him, but to all the children the monks were strange and alluring. Often they went in flocks along the path to the limestone tableland; they crouched in the chapel, out of the wind and the spit of the rain, to watch the fire burn beside the quartz cross or listen to the singing of the monks. One of them, by the name of Lua, would take the children to see the boat beached high up in a creek of red rocks. He let them clamber down into the boat and pretend they were rowing against a great storm or pulling up fish from the waves. So whatever the children understood, they knew the monks were generous, that they were kind and rarely scolded. Fian went to bed that first night knowing that somehow he had one of them all to himself. He wanted neither the grown-up world nor the world of his friends to know. He would much rather keep this thing in a box, a box to which he alone had the key.

The trouble was that often when he raced down the path to the edge of the sea and came to the place with the rock stairs that led to the beach, there was no Innis there to meet him. He crouched high up at the top of the beach, rocking on his heels and hiding his hands from the wind's chill, hoping and hoping. For he did not want Innis to think he had not remembered, that he did not care. That was an awful thought to Fian. And at night he was restless with worry over it; he did not know how to solve this first dilemma in his life. He worried at the knot in his heart until sleep washed him away, but even then he struggled and flung out in his dreams, for he did not want to lose this gift – this precious thing that was his and his alone.

That winter he was sick. Perhaps it was because of the strange thing he had eaten at the edge of the field, the thing with the stalk and the brown roof the others had dared him to eat. It had tasted sweet and good; he had not spat it out. He had forgotten all about it and had run with them to explore a new rock, to climb into a hidden cave, to come back by the edge of the sea where they were not supposed to go. Then all at once he had felt heavy and sick. He went to his mother but it was like walking through deep water, and the words he spoke sounded far away and someone else's. She carried him to the edge of the earth house and he closed his eyes; the cool of the place was good. When he blinked a strange orange colour came, and all he wanted was to lie there, still in the darkness, not talking or moving or thinking.

He never knew if it was that day or a day later or longer that he heard their voices. He cared about nothing but he was rocked endlessly on an orange sea and the sickness rose in him over and over. The voices came and went; they were muffled, and at first he did not even care about them – he wished they would go away.

I wanted the boy to learn. I can teach him.

His mother said something he could not hear. And he could not think of the other voice, or work out to whom it belonged. It was familiar but he could not think and he did not want to think. The orange wave rose again.

8

If you would allow me then I would. Please.

It was closer now, closer in all ways. Fian wanted to sit up and look but he could not; even the thought brought the waves back. And then he remembered; it was Innis! Innis had come to find him and his heart sang with joy. He had come to find him!

You can take him if you look after him.

The words washed him into a new sleep and when he woke again he knew at once he was not in the earth house. He was being carried out and he felt the wind about him; he was chattering with cold and he felt thin and sore. He was jolted this way and that, and he closed his eyes again, moaning because the sickness was so bad. It twisted in him, deep inside; like a snake it coiled deep in the darkness of him, thick and black. Then at last he was still. There was something warm around him and there were soft voices he could not quite hear. And then he drank water, the purest and coldest water that reached to the very edges of the darkness, and he sank into real sleep, good sleep, and the orange was gone at last.

*

'Come down with me to the beach. I want you to come with me.'

There was no wind, not the slightest breath. Yet still the low clouds were like torn shreds of wool over a blue sky. The light came and went, so full it was almost too much for the eyes to bear.

It felt as though the world was new, as though all of it had been reborn. It was as if he saw living things for the first time, smelled the roughness of peat smoke and had never done so before. His head was light and Innis went too fast for him in his eagerness; he almost tripped on a shard of limestone and had to stop, breathe, remember. The faraway hills were touched with snow. The winter remained, though he did not feel the cold. When the sun came, behind him, it was ice bright and cast clear brilliance on everything in its path. The monk turned, watching and waiting for him, eyes kind in that wide face. And the boy remembered that first moment he had seen him, his shadow reflected in the water.

He crept down the path to the shore like an old man, terrified of falling. Great trunks of wood had been brought in by the storms; every piece would be used by the springtime – not a fragment wasted. He tottered on in the end to the sand; Innis was waiting for him, carving letters in the sand with a stick. He crouched down and now he felt the wind; gnarled edges that ate the hands and feet with raw soreness. He could not endure this long.

'You nearly died, Fian,' the other said, and still did not look at him, still went on writing in the sand. 'But there was a plant we found, and maybe that healed you. Or perhaps it was our prayers.' There was the very edge of the sound of a smile in his voice. He put the stick down and looked at the boy. His eyes glittered over him before he spoke again and Fian met his gaze, waited.

'You will stay with us,' he said. 'You will stay with us and learn to write. All that time ago I saw what you drew in the sand and I knew you had a gift, Fian. I wanted you to learn. We will give you what we can and you will stay with us. If you are content with that.'

Fian kept looking at him, wondering. The words made a kind of sense, but they were too old for him and he was still dizzy and half-awake. Everything was new and strange.

'When do I have to go back?' he asked, searching.

'You don't, Fian,' Innis said, leaning forward and wanting to take hold of his hand. 'You can stay with us, for as long as you want.'

The thought stretched into the distance. A kind of sense seeped into his head, but it would take a long time.

'And I will teach you to write, Fian. To draw beautiful things.'

*

So he became one of them. His days were woven out of song; he wakened to song and went to sleep to song. He grew up fast, his head filled with stories of bread and fish, of miracles. Until then his small world had been a fight for space, for food, for attention. It had been a confusion of smells and dogs and voices. In the place of ghosts all was so much clearer, each day had the same rhythm. Yet more was expected of him, not less. In the earth house he had been a pair of hands to send out to the well for water; he had been a pair of feet to go and get kindling. Here he was the youngest of men; he was treated as one of them. And kindness lay at the heart of every command. There was no privilege in being the smallest;

11

he was expected to stay awake as late as all the rest. But it was the kindness that ran like a fine thread through everything, spoken or unspoken, and slowly he learned what it meant and how to give it back.

He had come to be taught to write, yet most of his days were taken up with learning everything else – about stars or the sea or the light that had come, or the songs that spoke of the light and the stories the light had brought. He had to know what words meant before he could write them. They had to mean something before he could carve them in the sand. The first word he wrote was the name of the light, and when Innis made the marks he made them with slow reverence. Fian watched his face as he wrote, and he saw the love in his eyes, the devotion. This must be the starting point, the beginning. And Innis talked to him there too. On days of storm they crouched in a cave out of reach of the sea in one of the arms of rock that held the beach. Innis talked to him about how words had come to be; the stories of words and sounds. For he had spent two years at a monastery, a place where many hundreds of them were gathered. Fian could not think what many hundred meant; where he had grown up there was nothing more than a cluster of earth houses. It was the only place in the world he knew, this headland and its coves and skies. Innis took him to the top of the hill and showed him the hills to the north that were still dusted with snow, and he said the monastery lay even further away than those hills, in a beautiful valley where the wind never blew and where there were apples and horses. Fian did not know what apples or horses were, but the words were beautiful, and he spoke them softly and let them roll in his mouth. And Innis wrote them in the sand for him – *apples* and *horses*.

What was strangest was meeting his brothers again, the whole flock of children he had been part of. They did not quite know what to do with him now, and although his first instinct was to run with them – to jump over things and shout and chase – he waited and was not sure. They gazed at one another, he on his side and they on theirs, and then they ran without him. For a moment he missed them, wanted to run and call for them to wait for him, and in his mind that was what happened. But his feet did not move. When he looked again they were gone; there was no sound of them.

Sometimes he missed his mother. He dreamed he lay close in against her and when he wakened the stone was cold. He whimpered sometimes and huddled in to his own sadness, but it was worst during the nights. She did not come looking for him or ask for him, and he knew that, he felt it. She was there, on the northern edge of his new world – she had not gone, but she was a shadow now. He grew into the new shoes of his life and they fitted his feet, they became all he had and all he knew.

He wrote in the sand and learned words hungrily; he felt there would not be space in his head for the number of them and yet that was the miracle – the more he learned the more space there seemed to be. He wrote them and saw them, but always Innis made him write slowly, carefully. He had to be *in* each letter as it was written; he had to live each one, as surely as he had to live the words of each song as it was sung in the chapel.

Yet every night the sea came back and washed away every word he had written. That was part of the learning too, to let go.

'For that is the story of all our lives, it is the one thing we cannot change. Everything we write in sand, and the sea will take it away. We cannot keep anything for ever. But you must still give with all your heart; you must not keep back because of that.'

The boy remembered his words when he watched the beauty of his drawings disappear one summer night. He had been alone on the beach and had drawn a tree, a rowan wind-bent and all stretched to one side, and among the branches he had carved things – harps and birds and half-hidden faces. And around the tree was curled a circle, a circle that was part of a letter itself. He went up to the top of the rocks to look down on what he had made and he felt a surge of pride, a beautiful warmth that flowed like honey through his whole being. And then the sea came and filled the first ridges of his circle, and then the tree itself was smudged. And he felt rising within him an anger that it had to be this way, and somehow he felt that anger was right, that anger and sadness.

When he lay down to sleep that night he thought of his picture and he remembered his father. He had not thought of him in a long time. There was nothing that could be done to bring things back, but did it not matter to grieve for them all the same?

*

He did not know if he believed in God. There were times he did – most of all when he swam in the sea. When the sea lifted him and he was held in the blue-green translucence, his breath caught by the cold, he had no doubt. He was held in the hands of

14

the sea and everything was in balance, there were no questions. But it was the passing of things; it was that which troubled him. Why had his father not come home from the stack? Why had they not all returned safe? In the cruelty of death there seemed to be no God. He asked Innis endless questions; he asked and asked until the young man laughed and held his hand, told him it was enough. But he looked back at him and could not laugh, he could not have that rock of calm certainty or serenity. He wrestled with the sea and there was neither victory nor defeat, just exhaustion. Only when he swam did he feel the knots of doubt and anger washed away, for as long as he was held in the hands of the sea.

'Am I a bad person, because I have so many questions?' he asked Innis one day. They had retreated from the beach to the little cave because of the hugeness of the waves. Innis had lit a fire, tiny and blown from side to side, that warmed at least the rawness of their hands. They fed the flames chinks of dry things from the cave.

'You are not a bad person because you ask,' said Innis, and there in his voice as always was the thread of kindness. 'Most people ask no questions. They have enough in this world to find food, to be warm, to find safety, to be loved.'

'Does God love them too?' Fian asked.

'Yes, I believe he does. And I do not believe he loves you any more because you ask many questions, or any less because you ask difficult questions.' His eyes twinkled and Fian sat in the shadows at the back of the cave, the words Innis had spoken like stones in his hand – trying to put them in an order he understood.

'I do not comprehend everything,' Innis said softly. 'There is more I do not understand than I do. But I will not understand by worrying or by lying awake at night.'

Still Fian searched his face.

'Imagine you were a tiny beetle crossing the floor of the cave,' he said. There was one, hurrying away from the fire between the two of them. 'You can know nothing of what the cave means, far less the sea out there. All that worries you is the fire and trying to escape it.'

He leaned forward towards Fian's troubled eyes. 'We are so small, Fian. We can only see such a small way ahead. But one day we will understand the cave and we will see the sea.'

It began to grow dark. They put out the fire and scrambled down the rocks to the beach. Fian did not know if what the monk had said had calmed him more than troubled him. The rain was sore on his face.

*

One night, one spring night, they sang not in the chapel but out on the limestone pavement. They sang there because the stars were falling; on every side there were bright trails of silver, little fires that shone a moment and were gone. A wind blew across the night, clear against their faces, but the beauty of the skies was too much – they had to behold it. It was a night you could see to the edges of the world; Fian turned all round and caught a hundred landfalls, each one of them crested with a sharp edge of snow. Even here on the tableland, a few footfalls above the sea, snow lay in the crevices and the stones were polished with ice.

'What do you think it means?' Fian whispered to Lua, looking right up into the blue-black night. A great white tail streaked down the sky.

'I think we will find out what it means,' Lua whispered back, bending to Fian's ear. 'I think tonight it means the world is special.'

It was almost midnight and still the boy did not feel tired. The dry wind blew around them, fierce, and as he held his head high he felt as though he was no longer standing but rather flying. The stars darted this way and that, and somehow he was among them, he flew with them. The monks sang on and on, their voices did not pause or break, and the words flowed through his head, carried him. He did not want this to end; he did not want to fall to earth again.

'How would you like to wait up and watch the dawn?'

He was so far away in his own thoughts he did not properly hear Innis' words at first. Nor did he realize that the others were drifting away now, still singing, departing to sleep. There were not so many stars now, just one or two, and they did not seem as bright as before. But still he was not tired; never in his life had he felt so awake. He turned and nodded, whispered his yes and looked back at the sky.

'The night is long,' Innis said, and the boy heard the edge of a smile in his voice. He said no more than that but led him over to a little knoll, a place to which Marua had always gone to pray. Marua who now could not speak; he who had given so much with his words.

They sat there, facing out west to sea as Marua had done, and still Fian's face was turned upwards into the sky. He saw the strokes of the falling stars and all at once they made him think of all that he drew in the sand, the letters and pictures. It was on his lips to tell Innis and then he stopped; the words froze and he kept them to himself. But it was as though a giant hand was writing on the cloth of the sky. He thought of all the stories he had heard of God and imagined this as another, that once in the crossing of the wilderness they had looked up and read the letters that were drawn in the sky.

Then the last of the stars fell and the sky was as always. Those that remained did not shine, they did not crackle and fire as sometimes they did – it was as though the heavens had been breathed with them. That was how Fian thought of it, like frozen breath. He shivered then and Innis drew him closer, brought his cloak around the boy's shoulder, and Fian was glad to lean close to him. The silence was neither long nor awkward; he knew in his heart he would remember this night for ever. His eyes grew heavier and he had to fight sleep, but the clear fierceness of the wind kept him awake. All at once Innis stirred beside him.

'Shall we go and write on the beach?'

They were not the words of his teacher but rather those of a friend. The thought had come to him all at once, from nowhere. 'Yes, all right.'

They would have run but everything shone with ice, it would have been madness. They went as fast as they could, together, against the wind, past the dwellings where the monks slept, out onto the path. The moon was like a piece of grazed ice in the sky, almost too bright to behold. Fian saw ahead of him the hills of the north, and he thought of the monastery where Innis had been, and he remembered apples and horses. Then they had started down the path to the shore and all of it was smooth and slippery. What they did was sheer lunacy, but that made it all the more wonderful to Fian. His heart hammered in the cage of his chest.

They came down onto the sand and it shone as clear as day. The tide was out; the waves broke and chased far below them.

'Will we work together?' Innis asked, and his voice was almost shy. For as long as Fian had been with them, the boy had copied and remembered what was written for him in the sand. Sometimes Innis had set Fian a task, had asked him to create a boat made from letters, or one single capital in the shape of a tree. But never had they worked together.

They drew a hall of men who sat at a long table. Around them in the air were mythical beasts. The men themselves and their table were perhaps in a strange ship that flew. Looking back, Fian could not remember who had thought of the idea; their imaginations had worked together to make the whole. And Fian was sure that the falling stars they had seen that night were part of the magic for what they drew.

He did not know afterwards how long they had been there on their knees under the white fire of the moonlight. Perhaps they were there all night, for when it was done at last and they crouched still in the sand he looked to one side, to the east, and a dark red stained the clouds – the first fire of dawn. And still they remained where they were, as the sea began to creep closer, the sea that would take their labour.

'Would you like to work with a book?' Innis asked, not turning to him and his voice soft. 'They need a scribe in the new land, a scribe for the book they are making, and I can teach you no more. I have taught you all I know and they have asked if you would come.'

Fian looked at Innis and still his teacher did not turn to look at him. But he saw the paths of the tears on his face, lit silver in the last fierce brilliance of the night. And he nodded, he said yes, he was sure. But he did not know why his teacher cried.

*

Innis sat before the other monks. The flame burned beside the cross as always, brittle and flickering but never put out. The boy was not there. He slept; he had slept for almost twelve hours. The snow had come back, flakes of it the size of lambs' feet. They came in flocks on the wind, came and went, leaving the pavement of limestone pattered with soft white.

'You know why we have called you, Innis.'

He blinked. He knew and he did not know. He still found this place a struggle. It wasn't like the monastery with its hundreds, the jostle and thrill of new learning, the books and the talk. This was a bare place; he loved them but their world was older, it moved more slowly and it asked far fewer questions. It was content with itself.

'I suppose I know that it's because of Fian.'

They nodded. He saw pieces of their faces in the light; pieces that shifted all the time. A frustration arose within him and he searched for words; he had to find and polish them before he uttered them.

'You cannot go with him, Innis.'

The words spoken softly, and even then with a thread of kindness. But now that only served to frustrate him the more, and the awareness he had not been allowed to speak. He knew they thought he said too much, that he thought too much. They stood together against him.

'And why may I not go with him?'

He would have said more but he stopped himself. Better this way, better than rage or grief. *Keep your voice sharp* – that was what he had been taught at the monastery. It was what he had taught Fian too, bless him, though how often did he forget with his torrent of questions?

'Is that not what you told the boy when he learned his letters in the sand? That he had to learn to let go? Now it is time to practise the words, Innis.'

He opened his mouth to speak but a new voice prevented him.

'There is another boy in the settlement who shows promise. We want you to begin to teach him. It is time.'

Now he did not know what to say. He felt helpless, even his anger had been taken from him. 'May I say goodbye?' he asked, his voice no more than a child's.

'No, Innis,' they said, and the two words flowed together – certain, final.

*

Even the dog did not remember the boy. It growled when he came closer and Fian drew back his hand, frightened it might bite. Smells and noises tumbled through his head. In the darkness someone moved and swore; a man's voice and then the crying of a baby. He bit on his lower lip, wondering if he should have come. He did not want to call; he wanted anything but that. Then all at once she was there and saw him, ten paces away in the grey of early morning, and he saw her eyes glitter over him. She waited.

'I wanted to say goodbye. I'm going.'

Her eyes narrowed to flint. 'You were gone a long time ago.'

She turned and went in to the darkness, was lost in the noise. But he heard her picking up a baby and softening its crying with her voice, and now he stumbled forward, never heeding the dog, and perhaps her name was on his lips, again and again. He was still twelve years old; he had had to grow up so fast.

And suddenly she was there again, the new baby cradled in her arms, and she had reached out to Fian and her face was wet. He held her and closed his eyes and remembered the day his father had not come home. She said things to him he did not properly hear but her voice was soft now, as sometimes it used to be, and that was enough.

The man appeared and he was wanting something and Fian found himself backing away, found himself almost falling over the dog. When he turned there was no one there. He went, chasing down the path towards the shore where the boat was waiting. When he glanced round again there was neither sight nor sound of the place.

*

He knew they laughed at him. They were easy with the waves; they threw commands about, walked untroubled as the sea rolled beneath them. He hid and shivered. The land reared up and down, swung away to this side and that; sickness was green in his stomach. The more he felt it the merrier they seemed to be; as the wind rose on the open sea one of them began to sing. Another of them came and asked him something and he could only shake his head; uttering words was too much. Innis and the place of ghosts, his mother and home – all of them tumbled through his head like waves, the sudden awareness that he was leaving and did not know if he would return, if ever he would return. He looked away into the bottom of the boat where none of those things would be and still they were there; he cried miserably, tasted the salt of his own tears. And the boat heaved and fell, heaved and fell; the boat did not care for his grief and the man went on singing, though the rest of them were silent, they no longer called around him.

'Drink that, boy – it'll heal your sickness.'

One of them had crouched beside him; his voice was different from any he had heard before. He sat up and drank; the liquid burned the back of his throat. He said thank you and sank once more from the horror of the heaving sea. He closed his eyes and held his head in his hands. He counted, counted from one to a hundred and then began again. He breathed, deep in and deep out. He slept.

When he opened his eyes again he did not know if he had slept a half-hour or a half-day. The boat still lurched about him but he was able to look now; the sickness had gone. He leaned against the side, low, so that his head and nothing more was above the boat. They passed through fragments of islands, a broken scattering of sand-covered beaches and hills, rocks that tumbled with waterfalls, inlets of seals. Sunlight broke white and sore from a place in the side of the clouds; for a moment the sea was too bright and he had to look away. The man who had come with the bottle passed close by and he was able to thank him. He was better and the water was calmer; this was more sheltered and he was grateful, with all his heart he was grateful. And he thought how small things matter, how small things change everything.

By the time they came in there was no sea at all and the skies were torn between blue and grey. He was being welcomed, his arm held, and then he was helped ashore. They were asking about Marua, about Lua, about Innis himself – their voices different and their voices the same.

The island was a soft green. It lay low and gentle in the water, its edges indented with white sand. The sun came and went; there was almost no wind at all. They brought him to a dwelling and he realized how empty he was, how much he had left behind. They told him to rest and they left him and he slept, dreamless.

*

He awoke in darkness, rested and calm. He heard soft voices somewhere close by and sat up. He was aware he had not eaten for a whole day; his head was light and strange, but something thrilled him – he did not feel hunger. *Everything was full of light.* Those were the words that came to him; he did not know from where. And he knew what he wanted; he wanted to write. Things moved in his hands and were alive. That was when they came best, through the night; sometimes there was so much he did not know where to begin and his hands shook with yearning to begin, to get everything down.

'Fian?'

Someone had seen him, was coming to find him. They had stopped talking and were coming to see if he was all right, and he smiled. He was glad he had said yes.

All those years and everything washed away. Now he could begin at last.

*

'Who are you?'

'The boy, sir.'

'Come closer. Closer.'

He went towards the thickness of a peat fire; though he was well enough used to the turf smoke of home, his eyes smarted now. He went forward and saw nothing as he went; his left foot stumbled on something.

'Let me see your hands.'

He held them out, shyly, and they were taken softly in those of the older man. Fian felt his own hands small then, yet did not quite know why. The others were so large and soft it was as though they contained no bones. Still he held them and seemed to study them.

'Yours are the fourth pair of hands.'

Fian looked up, bewildered, and he heard the smile in the master's voice.

'Three others have poured their love and light into the book, boy. Yours are the fourth pair, and perhaps the last.'

All at once Colum let his hands fall and Fian saw the edge of his face, as it is possible to see the edge of the moon on a certain night. Just the pale rim of it and the rest in shadow. There was silence and Fian heard the sound of his own heart; he wanted to speak for he was afraid of silence, and then he thought of writing in the sand, how there had been no need of talk then and of how he had not missed it. How even he had known it had been good that it was gone. He looked up again and saw the lit edge of Colum's face.

'There are times this will be the last place on earth you want to be, boy. When there has been storm for five days and no leaving your cell. When you have sat beside the same man to eat for years and feel you cannot love him any more. Or when your hands are empty and have nothing more to say.'

'And what is there to do then?'

Colum smiled at the impetuous tone. 'Go and find Ruach, even as I am telling you now! Go, be gone, get out!'

Fian fled, blind, out through the blue smoke, yet even as he went he heard Colum's laughter behind him. Had he passed or failed? He felt young and awkward and angered as he searched for the man called Ruach. He went to the stonemasons and they would not stop their deliberations over the markings on a stone for a long time. When one of them looked up at last he jerked his head in Fian's direction.

'I'm looking for Ruach.'

The man pretended to look under his bench and above his head and finally between the boy's legs. Then he shook his head extravagantly and returned to his measurements. The two of them laughed.

Fian went out with a face like a sunset and stormed off down a path. He almost knocked over the tiny man who was working the garden. 'Ruach. Do you know where Ruach is?'

The tiny man indicated that he couldn't speak. But he stood tall (and even then he didn't reach the height of Fian's shoulder) and pointed down away from the settlement and the chapels. Fian looked at him and understood that *might* be the answer, that was all.

The settlement was busy with laughter and talk and the barking of dogs. Fian decided he would follow the direction of the dumb man's finger and see where it brought him. He still smarted from the laughter of the stonemasons, and all at once he thought of his mother and brothers. He felt a warmth in his chest and he remembered her hand over his own on days when she had time for him and was not angry. He thought of Colum's words and felt he did not want to be here now, far less in another five years. By the time he had thought of all this he was out onto the rocks and heather and the talk lay behind him. He stopped and turned for a moment to look back, and then it came to him that he was free, that no one needed him at that moment, that Colum himself had told him, had commanded him, to find Ruach.

The otter played with the sea. It lay in a lagoon of blue water, and the sea was so slow and gentle it almost was not there at all. Once in a while a ripple passed over the water and it rose almost imperceptibly. The otter, lying on its back and fussing with something, rose all but invisibly too. And then, at once, like a thing possessed, it was careering about, under and over and through the water, so that Fian could hardly keep track of its movement. Just as suddenly, there it was on its back once more with a tremendous flapping of a fish, and the otter nibbled at it, the flapping held secure in its paws.

By the time it dived and was gone as though it had never been at all, Fian had forgotten the stonemasons and his hurt pride. He had forgotten too about home. He had walked a long way now, yet he did not fear he would fail to find his way back.

In a way he might never have left the headland where he had grown up. All of this was what made up the landscape of home: broken pieces of red-black rock, the curves of smoothed-out bays between filled with pure white sand. A huge sky that always knew the wind, and inland, glens of flowers that fought against it. On the horizon great grey tumblings of mountains, sometimes snow-shadowed and grazed on their summits. That was all, and it went on for ever. For all Fian knew, this was how the whole earth might be.

He remembered Ruach and started off once more, up and over a great long whaleback of hillside. Two ravens played in the clear air; they talked to each other as they rolled and fell. For a moment he wished like a child he might know what it was to fly. Then he forgot all of it and the ravens were gone as he saw the south coast of the island. The sun was on him and he had to raise his right hand to shield his eyes from its fierceness. All at once he wanted to run, and without thinking he began careering down through the heather, heedless of rocks and twisted ankles. He was a boy and he wanted to feel the wind through him. He liked to go so fast it felt faster than himself; he no longer knew what he was doing but he trusted his arms and legs. And he ran down into a valley.

It was a bowl of a place, surrounded by hills on all sides, except the one that lay ahead. He stopped, out of breath, his hands held at his sides. He felt something and did not know what it was. The sky above was pure blue, but there was no sun. There was something here that was not himself. It did not feel threatening; he would have stood in the same place at midnight with the whole fur mist of the stars above him and not felt afraid. He looked all around and there was no one, yet he felt a presence all the same. He felt healed.

He did not think it right to run thereafter. He walked slowly over the mossy grass and the bed of a small stream, up over the rise of a last hill and down onto a beach. A rubble of boulders first, then round stones as big as a fist, before smaller pebbles once more. The wind full in his face and the sea coming in like great white dogs, leaping and playing and breaking. He was so far away in the world of his thoughts he hardly felt the hand on his shoulder. He whirled round.

'So Colum sent you to find me.'

He had no time to answer before the man turned away to his left and suddenly bent down to the shingle and began sifting it with his right hand. Fian was saying something about having come the night before, about wondering where to find him, and all of it was useless.

'These are what I come to find,' said Ruach, and he held up over his right shoulder a stone that was green, meadow green with flecks of white. Fian took it carefully and it rolled into his palm. It was polished by the sea and when he held it up to the light it changed, became a little globe of translucence, orange-yellow bright.

Later they sat down in a gully out of the wind's knife. Ruach took out a handful of stones from a fold of his robe, and Fian gasped at them. They were green as moss and polished; one or two of them big as a thumbnail.

'Sometimes I can't sleep,' Ruach said. 'I have no rest for days and I know something is going to happen. I am certain that something is coming but I don't know what it is. And this is my hiding place.'

'But Colum knows you are here?' Fian asked uselessly.

'Yes.' The other smiled. 'And he has also sent you to bring me back.'

He got up and that was it. They started on their way to the settlement.

*

Why they woke him at night to bring him to the book he never knew. There was a wind that came from everywhere, that blew the light of their lanterns out over the sides of the path. There was a yellow patch of moon that darted through clouds, racing. Why had they waited until now, until the very middle of the night?

They climbed the stone steps and he heard the wind raging at the tower. It seemed to shake as they went higher, as they curled the spiral towards a top they never seemed to reach. They said nothing; his mouth filled with questions but always they fell to dust. He was frightened of being taken for a fool.

Then the room, and by that time his hands were paralysed with cold. They brought him over and he fought so his teeth would not chatter. They stood over him, watching not the page but rather him. It was beautiful. What more could be said or thought? It was all he had dreamed of seeing, since the days his hand learned to draw in the sand of home, since first he heard tell of books like this.

They said things to him then, over each other; that this work was his alone, that his hands had been made by God for this gift alone and he must guard them. He must care for them as a treasure of the Holy Spirit; he must not risk them or shame them. And the light of the lanterns fluttered and shadowed the page; the pools of blue and red, the dark and perfect script. Everything tumbled through his head and he was nodding, he found himself nodding and promising even though he scarcely knew what he said. And something hot touched his forehead and a cup was put to his lips and he drank. He coughed because of the strength of whatever it was, and he lost his breath for a moment; and then before he knew anything else they were bringing him down the staircase once more. They talked and if it was to him he heard nothing. He felt dizzy and was only glad when he reached the bottom at last and the swirling of the wind once more. And then, before he knew anything else, he was back where he had begun and the darkness was warm and he crept into the warmth of his bed. And all of it might have been but a dream.

*

'So, you are going further north, Larach? And what is it you are hoping to do? Find yourself?' There was a smile on Colum's face.

32

'No, I hope to leave myself behind. I hope to come to a place where there is nothing but God.'

'That place is called heaven, Larach. I fear you will be searching a long time for a place where you are not. But if you find it, come back and tell me where it is, because I would wish to go there too.'

There was silence and Colum turned away to the shadows and picked up something from the darkness. They thought perhaps he had gone for good but suddenly he was back, his full frame overshadowing them all. That was what they said: such a frame and such quiet.

'If you have come for my blessing, Larach, then you shall have it. I have been aware of your restlessness a long time, and that you are a navigator and that the sea is thick in your blood. I cannot know what you will find and you cannot know, but you will put your faith in the One who stilled the storm on Galilee, and that is enough for me. Have you companions to go with you?'

Larach nodded. 'Three, Colum. All of them have the same dream.'

'And what are they running away from?'

But now Larach was silent and could not answer. Colum's voice was mild, gentle as a child's. The question was straight and steady. 'I ran away too, once, Larach. So I ask myself the same question.'

'Perhaps it is the noise, master. There are men cutting stone and there is eternal talking, day and night. There are manuscripts being copied and there are scholars learning and discussing and arguing. Sometimes it is hard to listen to the heart. And that has weighed on me a long time, the desire to listen to my heart.'

Colum thought and was about to speak, and then he dropped his head and nodded. He nodded a long time and understood. There was nothing for it but to understand.

'I will miss you, Larach,' he said, and his voice was gentler still. 'I will miss your arguments and your struggle, your refusal to accept what you do not comprehend. But whether you leave yourself or find yourself I think it is right that you should go. If the noise is too great in your heart, then go north and find silence.'

'Thank you, master. I think that if I do return I will have learned to carry silence with me. I think all of us will have learned that.'

'If, Larach – if you return?'

Larach nodded, just and no more, and smiled and turned away.

*

It was a week later Fian woke and knew what was in his hands. It was still dark, the very middle of the night, and when he went outside there was nothing but the huge wind of the stars. And as he looked he remembered home and that night of gazing at the same stars, and how he had felt there on the edge of the monks' world. He remembered Innis. Was it any different now? Was he one of them or was it only his hands that were here? Was his heart elsewhere? And then he moved on into the darkness because he did not want to answer all that now. He wanted to draw.

He put wood on the fire and warmed his hands. It had sunk to an orange eye, a single globe that made no sound. It melted the twigs and he spread his hands before it, thinking of nothing and everything.

He had woken with the figure in his head, and he was afraid that if he waited until morning it would be lost. He had kept it and carried it like a living coal; he was sure that he could find it. Then he knew how it had been born. It was the otter, the knot of the otter in the bay that afternoon he met Colum for the first time. A symbol of eternity: a head that curled all the way into a tail.

At first there was a tremble to his hands; not fear that he would fail, it was not that. A desire of being certain; a desire to find perfectly. But then that passed; he flowed into a deeper self where nothing at all existed but the page and the finding. There was neither cold nor stone nor fire nor the wind that pattered against the stone. None of it was there; he flowed into the form and that was all. He had left himself. And by the time he had finished and returned from that place and shivered in the cold of the first dawn light, there was far more he had not known was to be found.

And that was where they found him asleep, curled over, when they slipped up the steps as the first red light seeped from the rugged eastern skies. They smiled and touched their lips and were glad, for they knew they had found the fourth hand.

So the island woke, and the bell tanged out in the quiet. A boat slid into the stillness of a bay to fish, and the arguments began once more among the scholars. The gardener who could not speak looked up, his hands thick with dirt, and praised God in the silence of his heart.

*

He first saw the girl one day when he was doing nothing. He had worked for hours, since the middle of the night, and his eyes felt hardly his own. It was strange to walk; he wanted almost to be down on all fours to be closer to the ground. And so he went, into the moor and the birdsong, under the blue skies. Over to the west he went, into the island's heart, and the larks rose up around him singing, and slowly his eyes were no longer strange to him.

It was as he crouched, there in the middle of everywhere, that he heard the girl. He heard her before he saw her; heard her singing and looked all round at first, not sure if he was dreaming. Because of the stillness of the day she was not close by and he knew she had not heard him. She was gathering flowers and sang to herself and he watched her, felt strange as he crouched there in the heather.

For a moment he feared terribly she would look up and see him and think he had followed her out here, for that was all wrong. So he crouched deeper, foolishly, as though somehow he might be invisible, even though his whole back and head were above the heather. And then he did not fear any longer, for he saw she was so absorbed in what she did she would not have seen him, or hardly cared even if she had. He saw the flowers she gathered, and realized he had not looked at them before. They were like candle flames: tall and white, the length of a finger. They did not grow everywhere, but rather in little villages, and he held one in his fingers, though he did not pick it. She had a basket beside her and laid those she picked in it, but she did not choose all. Some she passed over, and that left him the more curious.

So he felt courage and curiosity rise within him, and in the end he half rose, silent as a shadow, and crept round closer to her back so she would be in no danger of seeing him. She sang on; the same song, the same sweet, high voice. He crouched down deep once more, for all the world like a hare hiding from the hunter. He saw her face now as she half turned for flowers, caught the blue of her eyes and the gold-brown of her hair that rustled at her neck. And he felt a strangeness he had never known before in all his life, and then again came fear like a wave that suddenly, right then, she would know he was there and turn and see him. And he found himself praying, muttering a prayer that she would not and that he would not be discovered. So came the breeze and rustled the whole moorland; he saw it moving, saw the wind's hand strumming the blades and the flowers, and passing too like a breath through the gold-brown of her hair.

And all at once she did look up, and he barely breathed for fear that she would turn, yet she did not. The basket was all but full and she got up, slowly and strangely. She walked away from him, back the way she must have come and the way that he had come, limping and slow. And she sang no longer.

*

'Fian, what is the longest thing in the world?'

He shook his head, not particularly wanting to know the answer.

'A sermon on the evils of drink!'

He smiled, humouring them and hoping they might go away. But nothing is as funny as a half-drunk man, and the three youngsters had stolen as much as they could carry and were getting rid of it as fast as they could. One of them lurched and moved away once more.

'But can you tell us, can you tell us what the fastest creature in the world is called?'

'A saddle.'

'A saddle? Why on earth should a saddle be the fastest?'

And the three of them collapsed with laughter at the inanity of the thought. They cried until their cheeks coursed with tears.

'Dear Fian, won't you have some beer? It would cheer you. Just a little? Just one tiny glass?'

He shoved them away and went to the window. They had forgotten him already and were talking about their saddle. It was as funny to them as it had been before. And tomorrow they had to dig turf and carry wood, and horses' hooves would be dancing in their heads. All thought of saddles would be forgotten. He tried not to look forward to their pain and failed.

Who was the girl? What was her name and where did she come from?

*

He loved the scriptorium more than anywhere. It felt underground though it was not. The warmth of soft voices as they copied; the click and whine of the fire, and the rough blue scent of the smoke. The joy of what was being found and copied; the care over every letter and word. He read things that carried him away, that were beautiful with their talk of another world, and he thought what it meant to leave everything to follow this, to find something that could not be seen. He felt sometimes like a man who looked in from a night of snowstorm to a lit place of laughter and love. But he did not dare go in, or find the way.

'Come and read with us, Fian!'

The one who was nicknamed the Eagle for his nose called him over and they sat crouched, half a dozen of them, young and burning with the words. They read for no more than the pleasure of those words, and he crouched there too for a time and was carried away. But then he went out into the gathering night and the rain splintering the side of his face until it was sore, and he felt bitter and knew nothing. He loved the letters and the figures that lay in his hands, but the land that lay behind them – he thought he saw it sometimes like the magical land they spoke of on the sea's western edge, but then he blinked and it was gone.

That night he crouched by the window of the dwelling and was homesick. He wanted the soft hand of his mother in his hair, and her words when his brothers slept and she was content and without anger. Once at least he had folded his face close in to her breast and she had not pushed him away but told him a story, about a mouse that lost its tail. He could not remember how the story ended for he had fallen asleep, her hand still curling the hair at the bottom of his neck. He had felt safer and more content than ever before, and he never wanted to move from that place. But when he woke she had gone and his head lay in wet ground and she was shouting close by, raging about what she did not have. And he wondered as he got up if all of it had been a dream.

He wondered now, at that moment, if he should stay or leave. And he remembered Colum's words and thought how it was hardly the blink of an eye since he arrived. And he thought too of how his mother would scarcely welcome his return: she might reach out her arms to hug him on the first evening, but by the next she would be cursing the extra mouth that had to be fed and wanting him out from under her feet. What he wished for was impossible: to wander up the path home and be there with her for a few blessed hours, and then to slip away again before the sun's rim tipped the far hills.

'Fian, you asked about a girl!'

He swung round, embarrassed that he had been so carried away. It was Cuan, one of the young scribes, and he came in breathless with his hair to the four winds. Big-eyed and kind, he might be trusted to take gold to the furthest corners of the earth and not touch it. They sat together and Fian found himself again, listened.

'She is the daughter of a fisherman. She has a limp, for something happened to her when she was born, and she is sick. No one knows quite what ails her. And her mother is a healer. Why was it that you wanted to know?'

He clapped Cuan on the shoulder and smiled, shaking his head. The boy was like a puppy, eager and glad, with not a bone of harm in him. 'No real reason, Cuan. Thank you for finding out!'

But it made a difference that night in the darkness, as he lay and remembered her and wondered.

*

Sometimes the children from the island came and watched them. They gathered like a flock of lambs to look at the chiselling and the carrying and the arguments. They peeped their heads over the edge of the settlement wall and if anyone suddenly came too close they scattered once more, down over the rocky grass and away.

One day he took them by surprise and asked them if they would like to follow him. They glanced at him and turned away, and kicked their feet and bowed their heads, and he didn't know if they understood what he asked them. But when he let them decide, after he had gone down the hill from the settlement and the chapels, he saw them straggling after him, so in the end they must have decided he was safe enough. They had strength in numbers, and when he turned back smiling, they were coming after him.

He knew a tiny beach right below them on the east side. At low tide it was sheltered; a little boomerang of white shell sand that seemed never cluttered with seaweed and shells. That was how he found it now. He went down onto the sand and crouched, and he waited for them to come and find him. And he remembered Innis.

They would watch no nearer than the edge of the bank where he had dropped down. They twisted grasses with their fingers and laughed a little, shy and strange.

'I will draw something for you,' Fian said. 'I will draw you a boat!'

Then they came closer. As the boat grew and came alive in the sea that might have been real around it, they watched intently. They came down little by little, intrigued and held by the speed at which his hand moved in the sand, and he thought again of his beloved teacher and of all those hours of learning on the beach, and he wondered where Innis might be now. By the time Fian had finished, they had gathered close and were watching, but they took care not to touch a thing.

'I learned to do this when I was your ages,' Fian said, still kneeling. 'I had a good teacher and I loved to draw. It was the best thing in the world and it still is. That's what I do up there; I work on the book that will soon be finished at last!'

He watched them and thought of that gap between the grown world and the child's. He didn't know how to climb back; it was too late and he was too old, young though he really was. He smiled to them again and jumped up onto the bank and they scampered away and were gone. And suddenly he thought of the girl and wondered if he could find her, if there was any way he could see her again.

*

They woke him one night and it seemed to take a long time to return from the world of his dreams. He was asking them things in the shadows, as though he had travelled to the spirit world itself for guidance and was on the edge of hearing things, bearing answers back. He felt dragged out of sleep; up out of the depths towards light.

'Fian. Fian!'

And at last he knew that they were laughing at him, the circle of faces above his cot, and he wiped dribble from his mouth and was awake and embarrassed. They did not truly laugh at him; he was already too much of a friend for that. They laughed at his strangeness.

One of them, Neil, knelt down beside him. The dark curls shone. They were all scribes and they had been on the island several years now. They thought of little else: everything was the love of words, the creation of words.

'Come with us, Fian! Something has been brought here and we want to show you. Forgive us disturbing your sleep. But we wanted you to be there too!'

He rose and the cold was wretched. He still said almost nothing, afraid that the words he spoke might be nonsense. And they weighed

43

words. But once they were out into the cold rush of the night and the moon's fierce silver it was as though water was sluiced over his head and he was awake. He looked out east over the island that lay beside them; the long straggles of its headlands – and every rock was bright and clear. You could have walked the night through under that moon and never once missed your footing.

'What is it that we're going to find?' he asked, catching up with them.

'Wait and see!' Neil answered, throwing back a smile. 'Let it be secret till then!'

They left the settlement, walking south, and kept close to the shore. Even then Fian thought about the girl and wondered if he would see her again. Surely it was here she must live . . . Yet what would he ever say to her? And how could he even consider it when he had all but become one of them? There was no use in his wishing . . .

Then close to fields and over a wild scramble of rocks. The moon was gone a moment in clouds and he was more careful; he remembered their words that first night he was taken to see the book, and the promise he had made to care always for his hands. And suddenly they started down this rubble of boulders and grass towards the sea.

They went easily, as though they had been here many times before and knew their steps in darkness as easily as in daylight. He wanted to call them back for he stumbled and felt sure he must fall, but he let them go ahead and he picked his way, anxious and uncertain.

44

When he looked for a moment he saw a tiny inlet – nothing more than a jutting between the steep rocks – and there was a boat waiting. Fian came clattering down after them and they smiled at him again.

Neil clapped him on the shoulder and his eyes glinted. 'As well you work with your hands and not your feet!' he murmured.

And so they stood together at last on the edge of the rocks, and Fian's eyes followed them down into the boat. Two men sat there, one in each end, and two boxes lay between them. The boat thudded against the rocks and arms reached out to bring up the boxes.

'This is where I fear I won't trust your hands,' Neil said softly. 'What's inside is too precious. But one day you'll learn.'

Strange how they found a path he would never have seen, back up through the steepest of rocks. And it was slippery with slime yet not a foot wobbled, and then at last they were up onto high ground once more. Whatever it was they had brought with them, the men had been paid. Coins shone and were given once the boxes were handed safely across.

'Shall we put him out of his misery?' Neil asked on the plateau. 'Will we let him see before we send him back to his dreams?'

Not a box but a fortress. Layers and compartments and drawers; all made out of the darkest wood, and smooth. As he knelt he thought that it could not have been made by hands in Ireland; there was something other about it he could not have explained yet understood. Even the scent of it was from far away, exotic.

At last from the very heart of the box they brought out six vials made of glass. He had only seen glass once or twice before in his life, and these were squat bottles – dark also. Neil held one up to the moon in front of his eyes. He held it with trembling fingers. 'What is it, Fian?' he whispered. 'What do you think it is?'

It was as though all at once his tiredness washed back over him. He could not think and he did not know, though somehow he felt on the edge of knowing. Had it not been the very middle of the night . . .

'Ink!' Neil said, bringing the bottle back down, slow and careful. 'Ink from the other side of the world. For your book.'

*

'I have seen something,' Ruach said, 'but I do not know what it is.'

And there was a strangeness to the days, though was it because of the knowledge of Ruach's words, or was it really because they were strange? No wind; not even the grass seemed to stir in the fields, and there was always a breeze on the island – even if only the very edge of one. As though the world waited and held its breath; a single lark rose in the blue skies and twirled its song. The sea lay made of a single taut skin; it did not ripple and did not lap the shore. Ruach said in bleakness that there was no use in looking for green stones. Nothing would be given up by the sea in this stillness. He wandered about the settlement, slow and miserable, not knowing what it was that ailed him.

But it was the little dumb man that fell ill, the gardener, though who knew if that was what Ruach had seen. They found him on his side in the earth, scrabbling, and his mouth searching for words he could never utter. And it was as though they saw him for the first time. For he had been there but behind all of them, grey and silent. Now he occupied the centre and they brought him new good water from the well and held thimblefuls to his mouth. They laid him on a soft bed and fussed about him, wrapped him in layers even though the night was warm and the air still. Fian looked at that moment and he saw a strange red flicker low in the sky, and a few seconds later came the answering drawn slowness of thunder.

Then, as the rain began to fall outside and the heat broke at last, a woman walked in with a basket, and a girl was behind her. And the girl limped as she walked.

*

The woman sang all the time. She sang something that might have been as old as the hills themselves. It was beautiful, and to Fian's ears it told of the sea and a place in the sea. And he imagined home as she sang; a place close to where the monks had had their chapel, out at the wildest edge of the rocks.

The scholars and scribes fell away now as she sang; they stepped back and seemed to freeze, watching her and waiting. She and the girl sat the little man upright (though still he slumped over as though deep in sleep). She opened his mouth and put drops of liquid into it, and bathed his forehead and put something soft against his throat. This way and that she stepped, and always she sang, always her voice

47

carried through the chamber. And Fian noticed the scent of flowers; so strong was it he felt almost dizzy, and he remembered again the day out on the moor when he came upon the girl by accident.

He watched her now as she followed the woman, and he felt sure they must be mother and daughter. The girl kept her eyes always on the older woman; waited until she had finished what she needed to do and then let drops from another liquid fall on the tiny man's forehead and chest and finally his mouth. And the air became thick and dizzy with the scents, and suddenly and without warning the song was done.

'There is no more that I can do,' the woman said, turning to the monks. 'He may live and he may not, but there is no more that I can do. And now I am . . . I must go home.'

She sounded exhausted, as though all of this had drained her utterly. Fian thought she might fall even before she left the chamber, but the girl reached out and supported her. Both of them limped out of the shadows, and still not one of the men had spoken a single word. It was as though they did not know what to say, these men who rarely knew when to be silent.

Fian stood at the edge of the group, and suddenly it was as if he woke from deep slumber. He found himself chasing out after them into the warm night and the flicker of storm in the skies. He heard his heart chasing.

'Thank you for what you have done for Cuillin,' he said, and he was closest to the girl, and it was to her he looked as he spoke. He thought she smiled as she turned towards him, but perhaps that was only what he hoped. She seemed to think before she spoke; her words did not form themselves at once. And he remembered that there had been something other about her mother's words, as though she found them strange in shape.

'It was our joy,' she said softly, and the words were slow and different. 'We hope that he may be well.'

And then she turned away, and he knew that now she would be gone if he did not say something here, at this moment. He breathed and stopped walking; stood just there at the edge of the settlement. 'My name is Fian and I am working on the book.'

And he did not know what more to say. But she turned and now, even in the darkness, he heard the edge of her smile.

*

'They are in a dead place,' said Ruach.

It was the middle of the night and there was nothing but the *whoom* of the wind. A single candle struggled to live, there in the darkness between them. Colum stood at the edge of the cloister: there were no stars that night. 'But they are not dead themselves?'

'That I cannot say,' said Ruach. 'I only saw an island that was dead, but for fresh water. Living water that leapt from the very rocks.'

'It might be real and it might be metaphor,' Colum mused, and his shadow moved against the candle flame. Somewhere else, far away, the wind roared, and it came to Ruach that the wind could be many things in many places at one time. And he had not thought of that before.

'All I know is that Larach is the best navigator there is,' Colum said, and his voice was softer as he came forward to stand close to Ruach. 'We can do nothing but trust them to God. It is as though we must ship their oars. We cannot fight against the seas for them. We must ship their oars and trust them to God.'

'Is there such a thing as perfect trust?' Ruach asked, his voice soft.

'Perhaps not for us who have grown old,' Colum said. 'The child when he leaps from the rock into his father's arms below; he has perfect trust. But to learn it again when you have fallen and fallen, and when others have not been there to catch you – that is hard. I am not sure if we ever stop learning it, Ruach, that is for sure.'

The wind came again: a single huge boom. The candle flame hissed into darkness, yet still for a moment Ruach saw Colum there. 'I think he is looking for water. He is thirsty and searching for water.'

And there, nothing more than the shadow of Colum's head, looking up once more. 'No more than the rest of us, Ruach. No more than us all.'

*

The autumn had come. One day Fian got up and knew it. The day before it had been summer and now it was autumn. Nothing was different and yet everything was. He felt it and rejoiced, and did not even know why.

The day still, with pieces of blue in the faraway sky. The other islands lying in scattered fragments on a silent sea. The russet of the hills, and from somewhere the scent of smoke. He liked it that no one was about, that perhaps he was the only one that knew. And all at once he thought of Larach and his men at sea. Surely they must be dead, and perhaps that was what Larach had wanted. To find God in a storm's death. He had not wanted to fade into nothingness; he needed to fight against the lions and know that he had fought.

Fian went up the stairs, slow and silent. He felt there was nothing in his hands at all, but there were days like that when in the end it was enough to be here, to see the page and what had been before, to be set on fire by its beauty. When he felt a little faith he knew there was more to find within. It was strange, but on faithless days, especially when sea and wind tore at the island like a madman, there was nothing. He wondered what all this was, this fighting against the elements to do nothing but survive; this whispering of prayers and copying of books. Where was God in this grey world, and what God was it that toyed with them in the grey misery of storm? There had been days he had done nothing. Days when he had crept away and slept, when even Cuan with all his young laughter and kindness could not bring him back from where he had curled in against the wall.

Faith was for him a candle. It fought against the darkness, but sometimes it struggled and flickered; sometimes it was all but gone.

He sat there now in the shadows, his elbows on the cold stone. The fire clicked and he looked over into its heart.

'I came to find you.'

He all but fell to the floor with shock and she laughed. He turned and saw her now, coming out of the shadows, and still his heart chased. He closed his eyes and smiled, struggled to gather himself once more. 'You gave me a fright!'

He felt strange because somehow he was unprepared. He wanted to say something else but he had no words. He looked away.

'I am going to pick flowers,' she said simply. 'Would you like to come with me?'

That woke him out of himself. He was up at once and ready. She took a long time to struggle down the stone steps, limping all the time, but he carried the basket she had brought and was ahead of her, looking back and catching the gold-brown of her hair.

'It was on the moor I saw you,' he said, when at last they stood out in the limpid blue quiet of the day. Still the place was silent, as though all of them were in hiding or had slept far longer than was their wont. And again he was glad; he did not want to meet Neil or Cuan or any of the others. There would only be questions.

'I will go somewhere else today,' she said. 'It is the best place for the flowers I want to find. But you must be patient for I am slow.'

Her head was down as though ashamed and he wanted to say that it didn't matter, that it was not important. She said nothing but began walking, slow and steady out to the north side of the settlement. Then she began up onto the higher ground, and he thought that it must hurt her to walk here, but he was shy to suggest such a thing.

Instead he said: 'You must show me the flowers.' And at once he thought his words meaningless and foolish. 'I know none of them by name and I want to learn. I would like to find colours, inks, for the making of the book. Do you think that would be possible?'

She was silent a time and he dared glance at her, and he realized she was thinking. She thought about everything she said, as though she needed to hold and hear her words before she spoke them.

'I think there are one or two you would find,' she said at last. And he thought that she might say more but she did not.

Still they walked up and up, into rugged little hills with deep ditches and high ridges. She followed a path he could not see, right into the middle of the island where he had never been before, and at last they were high enough to see the other side and the west.

He looked back and the settlement might have been a cluster of child's toys. He caught the breath of turf smoke on the air, and he wondered where it came from.

They came to a strange high wall of rock and then curved round it and over. Now the west lay below them, dark rock and heather to the very edge of the sea. On and down to a place of wetness and a pool among the rocks. And flowers he had never seen before in his life.

'What is this place?' he asked, for it felt strange and he did not know why. She crouched down, the basket in front of her, and smiled.

'This is the Well of the North Wind,' she said. 'It is my favourite place. No one else comes here or knows of it. That is why I love it.'

And the words were beautiful to Fian, and already he wanted to find it in pictures. He wanted to find a colour to capture it, and somehow it was stowed away already in his hands, to be found when the time was right.

He gathered the flowers with her and they hardly talked or needed to talk. Sometimes the wind breathed about them but nothing else, and he was glad to be away from the arguments about angels, and the questions about the breaking of bread. For even his place up in the tower was not hidden away and silent. Nowhere was safe, except the hill alone where Colum slept and prayed. That was the only place. And suddenly he found the words pouring out of him without fear.

'Can I come here with you again, to find flowers and talk? Will you look for me as you did this morning?'

He watched her silence as she bent over towards the flowers, and it was as though her face broke and was glassy with grief. Her voice different and angry, sharp and shrill so he was taken aback, afraid.

'I am sick,' she said, and looked away from him. 'I am sick and I will die. I do not know when I will die and I do not want . . .'

Suddenly she had struggled to her feet and was stumbling away, weeping and enraged. For a moment he was so surprised, so taken aback by the shattering of the peace they had known, that he did nothing but turn and watch her go. Then he struggled up himself and was trying to catch her, wanting to stop her, wishing he had not spoken at all. She stopped at last on the top of a small hill and her face was white and cold, and she looked straight ahead into nowhere.

'I want to go back alone,' she whispered.

He nodded; he could do no more than that. 'I do not even know your name,' he said helplessly.

'Mara,' she said, and made its gentleness harsh and bitter. 'And I know your name!' And she began limping down and away home.

*

'I want you to go and find Ruach.'

What he wanted to do was to tell Colum about Mara, to ask him what he should do. He knew in his heart that either Colum would have sat him close by the peat fire and talked with him softly, or else he would have shouted at him and told him to be gone. There were no half-measures with Colum; he was either gentle or giant. And Fian feared he knew which it would have been that day.

Instead he stumbled out of the settlement south, the driven rain sore against his face. He did not want to go and yet he did; there was too much in his head for him to be still and draw. There had been nothing at all in his hands since the day at the Well of the North Wind.

He was soaked long before he came to the beach where he knew he would find Ruach, but it did not matter. He walked until he thought of nothing, and until his face was numb with the rain's sting. And he came down again into the strange bowl that lay up behind the beach, and even now he had to stop and listen to its silence. He remembered the first time he had come down into it and he felt no different now. It was like a green goblet, a chalice. There was no one here but himself and again he turned all the way round because he felt there was someone here, that there must be. And what came to him was the story of Moses and the holy ground – but why this place, and what burning bush was there to find? Had he seen such a thing then and there in the howl of the rain he would never have doubted again. And yet here he found it easy to believe all the same. And then something beyond his comprehension happened. A fold opened in the southern sky and for a moment sunlight poured down, into the green hollow itself. Of course not there only, but also. And it was as though a curtain was drawn over his doubt, and he was sure.

Then the cloud closed and the walls of grey were thick as ever, and even the green bowl seemed empty and nothing. Before he moved he asked himself if what he had seen had been real or a vision, for already it felt foolish and impossible. And yet he knew nonetheless.

A few minutes later he clattered over the first boulders onto the beach. It felt strange, thinking of talking now after what he had just passed through; he would have been grateful for time and quiet to wonder. But this was what he had been sent to do; he had to come back with Ruach.

At first he thought he was not even going to find him, that this time Colum had been wrong. But a sudden drifting of wood smoke made him turn his head, and he saw the gully of stone from which it came. He made his steps quiet on the stones; he did not want to seem to shatter Ruach's silence. He was a searcher too, one for whom the world was rough and jagged, as it was for Ruach. He searched for answers, he did not swallow them. And never would Colum shout at his doubting.

Now he was sunk over his small fire of sticks. As though he knew that Fian was there, he looked up at his shadow at the mouth of the gully and smiled. He smiled sadness, if such a thing was possible.

'You are wet to the bone,' he said softly, his brow furrowed. 'Come, sit close; warm yourself. Were it not for my folly and my dreams you would not have had to come the length of the island to find me.'

'I was glad to,' said Fian. 'I had stones to come and search for too.'

They crouched and stared long into the fire that drove this way and that in the wind. Ruach fed it, piece by slow piece, as rain was hurled around them in spatters. It came to Fian that never had there been another moment of light, and he was on the point of asking Ruach if he had seen it too. Then he knew he did not want to ask, for he did not want the answer. He was content with quiet.

Ruach smiled once more. 'This is the best time for the green stones, for they are made the brighter by the rain. But I have no heart for them, nor have I had from the first moment I came.'

'How long have you been here?' Fian asked.

But though he looked at Ruach for an answer none was offered. The other just gazed into the fire, his face deathly pale, and fed the tiniest of twigs to the flames. Had he heard him at all or did he not want to answer?

'I had a dream two nights ago, of a star that fell. It was bright and beautiful, and it fell into the sea. But because of the dark of the night, I could not see where it fell. But I knew that I had to find it.'

Ruach's mouth closed. He gazed still into the fire, as the wind came again and tore through it, driving the flames another way. Fian was frozen to the marrow; he yearned to leave and yet he could not say so. His hands hurt.

'That is why I came here, to know what the dream meant. And I am no closer, though I have walked and prayed and hungered and held myself sleepless since it came. Why am I chosen for such things?'

And Fian had no answer. If God wanted to give messages and truths, why did he not give them simply? Why had they to be translated, as though from some lost language? He had no answer.

In the end the last piece of wood was nothing more than blackened ash. Together they began the long march back, the wind rising about them all the time like ghosts, as the grey fell into darkness.

*

He dreamed of nothing but that it was cold, and woke and found it to be true. He curled in on himself, shivering, and turned and turned again in his search for sleep. He thought of the winter ahead; the long, slow drag of it, and his heart quailed. He had lost count of the days since he had drawn, and it was as though he almost doubted now that the skill still lay in his hands. But perhaps there was no more to find; perhaps the time had come to go home. But he did not know where that was any more. This was as much his home as anywhere.

In the end he fell into a half-sleep and he did dream, if dream it was. A girl sang as she fed a fire, and the girl was Mara. She had a beautiful voice and he wanted to tell her, but he lacked the courage.

When he woke it was with a start and his back hurt. And it seemed that in the shadows he looked straight into the face of Colum. And as he looked the face began laughing, rocking with laughter until at last it was still again.

'Dear Fian,' the face of Colum said, 'you have overslept. It is a new day.'

Fian drew himself up on his bed with shock and shame. 'Is that why you came here?' he asked, foolish and red. 'Was it to come and mock my sleep?' He looked everywhere but the face of Colum.

But the face of Colum he did not look at changed. The laughter fell away and the face became old and kind and full of a thousand journeys. 'No, Fian, that is not why I came here,' he said, and the voice was as soft as the nest of a mouse; there was neither mockery nor reproach in it.

'I am here because I have seen your struggle. I have seen that the page is dry and the pen empty. You struggle to find God and you will not let God find you. That is why I am here.'

Fian looked at him at last. He huddled there in the shadows, his knees up under his chin. He struggled for the words he wanted. How often would it have been easier to draw the words he sought than to utter them?

'Where do you find God?' he whispered. 'When you doubt?'

The answer came back at once, as fast as an echo. 'In the small things. In the voice of a child, in the curl of an otter, in the single moment of light on a day of storm.'

And he remembered the walk to find Ruach. He remembered and nodded.

*

And so was the night that Colum washed their feet. Three days it had raged like a demented creature; the sea threw itself huge and white over the headlands, and walking was a battle with the wind. What could hope to live out on that water? Hard to remember the days when it had been a single piece of glass, its edges all but unbroken. Now they huddled at the heart, in the place where prayers had been said so long it was as though they had made smooth the very stones. They held together and heard the roaring beyond them. They did not want to be afraid and yet they were. And all that day they were hungry and barely a word was spoken. Everything they were seemed in doubt, became distant and lost.

And then in the evening it dropped; they heard that it fell, just a little. And the bell rang; they heard it over the gusting of the wind. And Colum was suddenly with them; he sang soft and low, and his voice carried among the stones, so that one by one they seemed to waken from a kind of slumber and sing also. Until all their voices were as one, and yet still they were soft, but stronger than the storm. And then Fian saw what Colum did – or rather, he heard the sound of the water first, and understood when he looked. Colum washed their feet: from eldest to youngest, from wisest to slowest – tenderly and gently he washed and he dried their feet. The feet too of little Cuillin who had almost died, who smiled shyly as his master cared for him and loved them all.

*

'Fian, you must come with me!'

It was the first time he had slept well in days and someone was dragging him awake in the middle of the night. He said things that

61

made no sense and found himself on his feet, scrabbling to wrap his shivering. The voice that had called him again and again talking endlessly now about what he could not understand, and then they were out into the night. The wind had no longer its first force; it was not constant but it gathered its strength and came in great sudden booms. The night was starless and moonless, and suddenly at last Fian realized it was Ruach who had pulled at his sleep, chattering nonsense as he dragged him along now. All at once Fian was awake; he held Ruach's shoulders and shook him.

'Enough! What is it? What is it you have seen?'

Ruach reached out and held him, like a little child. And Fian stooped, for he was taller than him, and Ruach's mouth whispered against his ear. 'I don't know, but there is something I have to find!'

There were a hundred things he could have said, yet it was that trust which made him say none of them. Ruach had sought him out and that he could not reject. But if they were to search the darkness then they needed light. He found a lantern and he found Ruach once more. 'Where do we need to search? Do you know anything?'

The face grey and pathetic. He was like a dog that has been whipped. Eyes that did not know where to go. The wind roared against them. 'The sea! All I know is that. Somewhere in the sea!'

He was awake now and enough that his sense of humour had returned too. He wished he could tell Ruach's dreams to be a little more precise. If they searched the next ten years, that might not be enough.

They went uselessly down below the settlement first, close to where once he had drawn in the sand for the children. They staggered about like two drunk men and Ruach held onto him, half talking to himself all the time. Fian wished that this might be enough to satisfy him, to let him see there was no point. But then Ruach was not like the others, and when a dream haunted him nothing would heal him until it had been understood.

Two things changed, and more quickly than ever Fian would have imagined. First, the wind eased, almost as though it had grown tired of itself. And it grew light; or rather, a pitiful grey band brought the ghost of the morning to life. Not life exactly, but to some state beyond death. It was freezing and the last of the wind was a jagged edge of knife that bluntly tore at face and hands. But it was a kind of dawn.

Fian let Ruach lead the way. Ruach did not know where to go, but he staggered north, hugging the coast. It was tiring beyond words; they hardly went any distance before a new wall of rocks loomed ahead, slippery and brittle. Ruach fell again and again; it was now light enough for Fian to see the bright blood on his hands. But always he picked himself up once more and went on, the sunken eyes searching and searching for what something deep inside had seen.

Then, just when they had all but reached the north end of the island and were about to step down onto a long curve of white sand, Ruach pointed. He let out a half-cry and staggered down over the boulders and down. Fian followed. He saw something ahead but had no idea what it might be. He caught up with Ruach and they ran the last of the way together, where the tide was coming shining over the beach.

A boat: the broken remains of a boat. And a man: the broken remains of a man. And Fian recognized him as Ruach was down on his knees already bringing him out. It was Larach, and this was Ruach's fallen star at last.

*

They were fragments. No, they were the broken pieces of things that once had been fragments. Larach came and went; like a man deep underwater he came up sometimes, for a moment, to the surface, and his eyes opened. A word, a few words, and then he was gone once more, back into the soundlessness of the deep, from which no one could reach him.

They watched him night and day in shifts. Even Colum, for Colum loved him like a son: there was a bond between them no one could have explained, least of all they themselves, that was real enough for that.

Sometimes he fretted in his sleep; as though wrestling sea creatures, his hands fought. And he struggled where he lay; glistened with beads of hot sweat, and they held him until he calmed and cooled, until he fell under the surface once more and was gone. When he slept then it might have been that he was

64

dead; his breathing thin, almost invisible, and his eyes still. Day after day after day.

And after however many of those days she came, with her daughter. They had not even told her of Larach, had not sent for her – yet all at once in the evening she was there. Had someone told her of the finding of the ruins of the boat, or had some deeper voice told her of his need? Fian was there when they darkened the door. He felt a shyness through him he had forgotten he possessed; she had not come to find him, and she did not even glance at him, and yet he followed her every look and move, felt his own face and hands strange and awkward.

'There is nothing I can do for this man,' the woman said after she had knelt by him a long time. 'I cannot bring him back from the place where is gone; he alone must choose. He has many dark dreams; he has seen things he yearns to forget.'

And all she did was to drop sweet oil on his face and forehead, for his skin had been dried crisp by the sea. She smoothed it into his skin and hands, tender and slow, and the scent of the oil filled the chamber like an enchantment. Then she and the girl were gone, as suddenly as they had come. And Fian looked at the girl as she left; he had not meant to, he never intended to, but he could not stop himself. Yet she did not look at him as she vanished.

The only one who slept and slept, deep and untroubled, through those days was Ruach. Even his face had changed; the mask of fear and torment Fian had seen that night, the night they found the boat and Larach – it was as though it had never been. Blessed in calm it was; his hands nestled by his side, and the curl of a smile on his lips.

Poor Ruach, Fian thought tenderly as he passed him – *at peace until the next dream comes to haunt him. And just what did God mean with that?*

*

It was calm after those terrible days of storm. A flickering of snow on the highest hills of the closest islands, and the skies clear and still. The geese came in their arrowheads, and Fian closed his eyes to hear their voices. They brought the winter but he loved them just the same.

Suddenly there had been many things in his hands, after the night that Colum washed their feet and after the finding of Larach. It was like drawing down a bucket into an old well, one that long had been dry, and finding to one's utter surprise there was water in plenty. Yet he knew now that he believed things came from his hands. He could not explain it, and perhaps it was good he could not, yet he knew it was true all the same. And the God that Colum had spoken of – the God of the bright moments – that God he could believe in and love.

'The sun did not go below the horizon at midnight, and the land was still awake – the birds called and there was life, life in all its fullness.'

He ate bread; he ate bread and drank milk. Quite suddenly he had come back, as though indeed he had decided the turning in the road he must take. Thin as though the sea had washed him away, had worn him to no more than sticks that might break in the slightest wind, and yet he was there. Larach, the only one of the four who had returned.

And Colum crouched closest to him now and listened and watched and nodded. And Larach smiled and said he did not want them to sit there and see him, but they sat there just the same. He was their brother and they had prayed and he had come back.

'What happened?' Colum asked, his voice low so it was almost a whisper, and he was the only one who would have dared to ask.

Larach sighed and his hands held each other on the bed, and Fian saw for a moment a greyness that crossed his face, a flickering of fear, that he thought must have been the remembering of terrible things. Larach swallowed and swallowed.

'We went north and there was nothing the first days. It was good and we landed in a place of trees, made a fire, drank water.'

It was those words that stopped him, that broke him. *Drank water*.

Grief swelled in his eyes and the tears coursed his cheeks; the thin frame of him shook and he brought his hands over his face, ashamed they should see. They spoke to him, rocked him, hushed him like a child.

'Later there was no water,' he whispered. 'There was thirst and no land for days, and I thought things that make me ashamed.'

They let him sleep then and it was as though for a time he fell back into that deep place of water. It was a dark pool, and though it was on the edge of death it was not death itself and it was beautifully tempting. There was no fear there, there was nothing but nothing. And all that long night he slept.

Around him they worked for the winter. They built walls against the winter. A boat came from Ireland, with news and fresh meat. Fian thought then of how far he had come since he first left. He could never have gone back now and he would not have wanted to.

And he did not miss them. That truth stabbed him sharp and clear. *He did not miss them.* He thought how his mother would misunderstand this world and want to be gone. He would show her the book and she would stare at him and it and have nothing to say. How did a book help with the washing of children or the making of food?

'Aran died. He drank seawater because he could endure the thirst no more, and his lips and eyes turned black, and in the morning he was dead. I would not have known his face again and now I cannot forget how he looked in the end. May God grant that one day I can forget.'

And a murmur passed round them as they huddled that night to hear Larach's story. He had walked for the first time that day, in the sudden frost of the morning with the skies blue-white and the hills sharp with their edges of sunlight. Two of them had helped him walk, as though he was an old and feeble man, not the strong navigator he once had been.

'We came to an island ten days later. Sharp and high it rose out of the sea, like a creature that had frozen to stone. Barren it looked; a place of blackness and emptiness, yet we dragged the boat ashore with what little strength remained, and then the miracle . . .'

Even now, Larach's eyes glistened and he turned away a moment and Colum leaned to reach his hand, to murmur words of strength. But he found his courage again, turned back and now his voice held.

'The sweetest water I have tasted in all my days,' he said, 'from a pool like a font in the rocks. As though it had been prepared for us, made ready a long time before. We drank and we drank; we covered our heads and faces with water, we laughed and we rejoiced.'

His face changed and the eyes darkened. 'And we thought of Aran, how he should have lived that little longer and been among us.'

He waited, and his eyes glittered over them, and not an eye or hand moved. 'We stayed there two days and two nights, and then we started north once more.'

They saw it, the painting of the voyage he had made for them. There in the winter darkness of their world they were back with him. They did not want to sleep until they had heard the story to the end.

'We came to a great island, were washed ashore onto a black beach. All the stones and even the sand – black. I think we slept where we lay. It was not cold but we woke again in the rain, and then we found a cave – deep and warm and sheltered. The first thing that Rua did was to paint a cross on the stone wall – and to carve the cross that he himself first made here on the island! We stayed there a long time, for we were weak and perhaps afraid.'

The wind came now and pulled at this place of sanctuary, and Larach fell silent. His head fell and all of them sat crouched, listening, and were there in their minds in that island cave – waiting and wondering. And in that moment of silence, that very moment, the cat called Pangur came miaowing in to their midst. And they burst out laughing – all except Larach perhaps – and the laughter rose until Pangur herself had fled back out. Even then in the end Larach laughed, there where he sat, and Colum beside him. The cat had broken the spell.

'Enough for tonight,' Colum told them, 'and tomorrow there will be more!'

And they went out into the bright blue beauty of the night, the skies blown by a huge wind, and a few stars not sharp but like grains of salt. And there was something of Fian that almost wished he had gone, that thought he should have had the courage. And then he remembered what an old man had said in the place where he had grown up, that it was all very well to say you were steady in a storm when you were sitting at home in the rain.

*

Colum was ageing. Fian thought of it that night; how he did not hear so well, and grew cross at things he could not mend. The man

70

he had been lay inside, and often – especially when they gathered to sing – was no different. He was the Colum who had landed here to change the world. He was as strong as on that morning they had dragged the boat ashore and a new life had begun. But sometimes, just sometimes, Fian caught glimpses of an old man. A man that was tired, who had carried too much for too long. But he would say nothing. He would have no help, no pity. It was a brave man that asked, and an even braver one who asked a second time. He spent time alone and came back strange and distant, as though he had sought to find himself and been on a long journey. Fian thought he would have liked to take that great hand a moment and hold it tight, as though to say many things that could not be uttered with words. But it was not for him to do; it must be one of the others. Yet he wished it might have been him all the same.

*

He woke during the night and was quite awake at once, knew that he had slept enough. There was something in his hands, almost a tingling; something was buried there that had to be found. He got up in the dark stillness and crept outside. The night was blue and his breath smoked away into nothing as he stood there yet. There was a pattering of snowflakes on the wind; they came, thin and drifting, and melted wherever they landed. All around him the others slept, and that was good. He had always liked to be the only one awake and he never quite knew why. As though now he stood on the edge of some great find, that he alone was awake for a reason. He made not a sound as he moved through the settlement and went into the tower. He remembered the first day.

Yet perhaps he had been wrong. He sat a long time in the darkness and the silence, and what was buried in his hands remained hidden. All he knew was cold; the wind came in ghosts and was gone, but he shivered in the end and huddled in to himself over the page, and thought bitterly that it would have been as well to go on sleeping.

Until dawn. Until the sky above the far island became like the belly of a fish, flecked with strange fires and patterns. He stood and watched for a time, until he understood. It was that moment of light he wanted and had to find. He went back and began, and then, as always, time ceased to mean any more. He might have been there an hour or a half-day, and all the cold and hunger and doubt was gone from him as though it had never been. There might have been voices around him too; Neil or Cuan or one of the others. He would not have heard them. All he searched for was the finding of the light.

When he was done he drifted into a half-sleep but once again he would have had no earthly idea how long it lasted. All he knew was that in a dream he saw Mara before him, coming closer in the shadows and speaking his name. She spoke it again and looked at him, but her voice might have been underwater and he could not answer.

'Fian!'

He sat up and he realized that it was no dream at all, that Mara herself stood in front of him. And he did not feel strange, as on the night when Cuillin had been healed. There was no time for that now.

'I brought you something,' she said, and held up a tiny vial. 'It is a colour, a colour I do not think you know and that has no name. But it is made from flowers on the island. I hope that you can use it.'

She turned to go.

'Please, Mara – wait!' he implored her, and she turned back to him. He remembered the last time he had seen her, at the Well of the North Wind. He was afraid he might say the wrong thing again now, but he had to speak. Her face was gentler; it was not torn and anguished as it had been that day.

'I am better,' she said, as though he had asked her, 'but the winter is long and hard to me. There are no flowers and I miss them.'

She smiled and he nodded, understanding. He had never thought of such a thing and yet it must be so. The same eyes see different things, he realized, and that was somehow strange and even wonderful.

'Thank you for this,' he said, and he went to the light of the window and held the vial there so he could see the colour. How many thousand flowers had been melted into those few precious drops? She went over to the book to look at his page; he heard the uneven steps as she limped over the stone. He was pleased that she looked; he wanted her to.

'It is beautiful,' she murmured, and that gave him courage. 'Will you come and visit us?' she asked, as he turned from the window. 'My mother would like to meet you.'

*

It was dark and low and he felt shy. He felt still in a dream that Mara had come to find him and bring him a gift, and her mother did not smile but looked at him a long time and then took his hands. She took both of his hands and turned them upwards and studied them. Then Mara brought candles and he scented things he had never known before, and she offered him something to eat.

'You are a good man,' her mother said to him, dropping his hands at last. 'But there are things in your hands that are dark.'

Then she was gone, away into the shadows, and Mara leaned close. 'She means no harm. She wants very much to see the book!'

'Then she must come and see it!' Fian exclaimed.

A man loomed out of the dark and took Fian's hand and all but crushed the bones. He carried a net with him, said nothing, and was gone.

'My father,' said Mara, her voice quieter. 'He is getting ready to leave for the fishing. But he does not understand the language you speak.'

'Then how did you first learn?' Fian asked. 'If it was so strange to you?'

'My mother learned from the monks when they first came here. She wanted to learn what it was they brought; she was curious. And then when I was growing one of the monks came to teach my brother and me. My father did not want me to learn at all, but my mother made sure that I did. Sometimes she helped me. When we

74

were walking for hours to find flowers she taught me words. I still have much to learn.'

'You speak well,' said Fian, but he uttered the words softly, for he thought she might not want her father to hear them. The fire was stirred and his eyes smarted with turf smoke and he thought of home. He remembered how he had learned to write against his mother's will, and he found himself telling Mara, and about how he had been brought here.

'You know that your book will have to be hidden,' she said, and he thought it strange, as though she had heard nothing of what he had just told her. He neither nodded nor shook his head, but looked at her waiting for her to say more.

'My mother has seen it,' she said at last. 'She has seen men from the north who would steal it. One day it will have to be hidden.'

And he in turn did not know what to say to that. But he knew Ruach and he knew the power of his dreams. And he thought of Larach.

'Then the book must be kept safe,' he agreed. 'It is precious, more precious in a way than gold or silver. It is a thing without price.'

All at once she leaned towards him and spoke soft and swift. 'You must go now. My father is getting ready to leave and I know he will want me to help him. Come back and find me – at midnight.'

He found himself outside and his head felt such a tumbling of words and strangeness. But that he had seen Mara again at all; that she had come to find him. He saw a boat nodding on the water; heard the voices of men on the shore. They looked round at him and he felt shy; they did not greet him. He was from his world; they from theirs. And he thought how it must have been when Colum first came here with his stories of a man who had died and returned from the kingdom of death. What did they think of Colum, these fishermen who had been born here and who would die here? What did they think of his chapels and his crosses, of all those who had come here in his wake?

He could not work the rest of that day. He was restless and his hands would not be still. He talked with Neil and found himself irritable and short-tempered. He complained about wood and light, and afterwards as he stormed away towards his own shelter he wondered where his frustration came from. Was he just tired? Was it as little a thing as that? He almost hoped it was not, that there could be more reason for his mood. But if there was, he had no idea what it might be. He thought that Ruach looked anxious, and worried that a new dream lay like a shadow over his heart. But if it did, he was not the one to solve the riddle.

He did not know what to do with himself. Had he tried to sleep he would have thrashed the hours away, searching for the best place to lie. He found little Cuillin, working away at the ground despite the frost, and saw the child-like joy of his smile. He had almost nothing, yet what he did have he loved with all his heart. Fian felt ashamed of himself for his bad temper, and knew that he should go back and find Neil and tell him so. Not that Neil would bear any grudge; Fian's grumbling would be like feathers in the wind to the good-hearted Neil, who found laughter everywhere he looked.

No, he did not go back to find Neil as perhaps he should have done. He went to find Ruach, and he knew where he would find him.

How silent it was, the island – like a creature that had crept underground to sleep the winter. There had been frost the night before, and pieces of ice lay white across the moorland. No more than fragile flakes, so that when you held them they were gone in a moment, turned to a trickle of water.

Fian looked out at the broken pieces of island that lay all around them, as he had often done before, and asked himself if anyone lived there. He knew of some monks who had gone to set up a chapel and a settlement on the nearest island, for that was what Colum wanted. He had never intended they should remain with him, copying manuscripts and arguing over angels – he had wanted them to leave, to set off on new journeys, carrying with them the story he had brought from Ireland to share like bread. In the beginning it had been like that: plenty of them had been set on fire by his passion, had all but thrown themselves into boats to do his bidding. But that was a long time ago, years before Fian had known him. Now he was gentler; the fire in him had not died, it had become a glowing heart. Now he did not want those around him to be gone; he wanted them to stay.

Fian saw a seal head dark in the waters of the west side. He could not resist going closer, as he had never been able to resist since childhood. The seal swirled about the shallow water, vanished sometimes until Fian was sure he must be gone, and then magically reappeared somewhere else entirely. Fian went out to the edge of the rocks and waited, feeling twelve years old again. Neil, Colum, Cuillin, even Mara – all of them were for a moment forgotten.

The head appeared in the water and the eyes studied Fian for a moment. He crouched in the rocks and sang, his voice strong and steady, for he had heard stories of seals coming close to hear the singing of humans – there were even songs written to bring them close, though he had never heard them, far less learned them. His mother had had no time for such things.

He thought now that he had sung rather well, and he looked to see where the seal was. After a moment he could not help but smile to himself, for the seal had disappeared. It was a sore lesson to learn that day.

He set out across the last hill and came down to the green dell, the place where the light had shone that day of greyness. And now there was nothing; it was empty and silent and no more than a place held in the hands of the hills. Yet that in a sense only confirmed what he had felt before rather than anything else. It made it easier to believe, not harder.

'You did not just come down to find me, you came to find yourself!' said Ruach, and there was almost a smile as he spoke the words.

'I came to find many things,' Fian agreed, and he started sifting in the piles of shingle about his feet, in the hope of a bright flash of green.

'What is it you have seen, Ruach? Do you know yet?' He would not have asked had he felt that the man was too deep in his inner turmoil. Perhaps now he felt he knew Ruach better than any of them, liked him even more too. He wrestled with light and dark, and was not afraid to show it. No, that was not true – there was little he could have done about showing it – there was no choice. But Fian had seen too much show, even among the monks, and nothing had made him doubt more than that. Ruach struggled, yet he did not let go. Year after long year.

'There was no dream,' said Ruach, and he looked out south as he spoke. 'Sometimes it is like that. It is as though I am given a rock while I sleep. I can feel its shape and size – I can see it. But I have to translate it. It has come in another language and the languages are never the same twice.'

'I think I told you that sometimes I waken with things in my hands,' said Fian. 'Drawings. And I don't know what they are until I go back to the book, until I lose myself in the work. I have to lose myself first.'

'Perhaps we can exchange dreams,' said Ruach, and again a shy smile curled his lips. 'I would not fear yours quite as I dread my own!'

'So how do you find it in the end?' Fian asked.

'For every one there is a different answer. There is no learning how it will be next time. Always I pray, Fian – I pray that I may know quickly and be spared the torment of the searching. And I never am.'

'Why do you think that is?'

'It's what I've been given to carry.'

No voice of martyrdom. The words just as they were, neither heavier nor lighter than that. And Fian nodded and could say nothing more, and the two of them crouched there for all the world like two boys, sifting the stones for green treasure.

'Once I asked that it might be taken away,' Ruach said in the end. 'I thought I could never go through it again. Perhaps it is like going to sea, knowing always you will be desperately sick. You know it is ahead of you and so you dread everything. You dread the next time. And then I dreamed that I had been given a new boat. Not only that, but I was a child again. I was not this failing man I saw in my reflection; my skin was new and shone. I knew that the boat was a gift, and I ran to it with a whole heart. And ever since then, it has been different.'

They did not come back together, for Ruach was not ready. Fian came alone, slowly, and he thought of the dream the whole way over the island.

*

It was a struggle to wait up until midnight, and a struggle also to escape from people. This little island could be a babble of tongues! That was what Colum had once shouted in fury when he could find no peace to think, and there were plenty of days it was true still. Often enough it was exciting talk; two young men wrestling with ideas through the night and not sleeping until the dawn had crept in over the sea; others carving songs, carving stone, carving wood – and talking as they did, searching their way forwards.

He wanted to slip away like a shadow long before midnight, and of course they did not want to let him go. The place was busy and excited and he loved it; just that that night of all nights he wanted to be away.

'Stay with us, Fian, and tell us what you think! You spend too much time on your own, hidden away in that tower! There are times you need talk, too, and you need us! Stay with us and tell us what you think!'

He promised it would be tomorrow, and they shook their heads and smiled.

'That story has been taken out of the drawer once too often,' said Neil, though they knew they were beaten. 'We're just not good enough, that's what it is.'

'I shall swim round the island twice over in penance if I don't keep my word,' said Fian, and that was enough to have them raise their eyebrows. He heard their good laughter as he went out into the darkness.

A full moon that night and a silver light poured over land and sea. Not the tiniest breath of wind and the sea silk. He was not cold, though he thought that by morning there would be a glitter of ice on the stones.

It was a miracle to have escaped, he thought. Harder to explain his wanderings tomorrow if they went to find him in the tower that night and found neither his candle nor his bent head. But tomorrow would have to take care of itself. He left the settlement and found his path, was thankful for the moonlight. He could move swiftly enough and not risk a twisted ankle; every step was clear. He got there and Mara was waiting outside; she put a finger to her lips and drew him away from the doorway, whispered to his hunched shadow.

'My mother is sleeping! As long as she doesn't hear us now . . .'

She took his hand and led him, down and down to the shore. He had thought of it before and he thought of it now, how humans could be so quiet when they pleased. They could make as little sound as deer.

He was shy that she took his hand and yet he liked it. When they reached a path through the heather she let it drop again and he was sorry, but he would never have had the courage to reach for hers again. The moon might have been leading them, and making a path across the sea that was almost unbroken. And he wondered where she was taking him, and at midnight, and she walked quickly despite her limp – up now over a headland and a long plateau of grass. Still she did not walk beside him but ahead, and the tiredness he had felt earlier was gone. There was a gladness in him, a glow, and now they were going down onto a curve of beach, but walking on to its end and up – to a steep slope of rock and ivy and a single wind-bent tree. Up at last to the shallow arch of a cave.

He sat beside her and understood nothing, but he did not want to ask.

'Look,' she said, and he stopped looking at her but at what lay in front of them. The curve of beach stroked by the sea down below them; the far island and its headlands, its great hills – all lit by the ball of the full moon that lay right ahead of them. Never had he seen its grazings and its silver pools so magnificent, and their faces were bright with its shining.

'I knew it would be like this tonight and I wanted you to see it,' she said.

'I'm glad I was able to escape,' he told her. 'They were all excited and wanted me to stay, wanted me to talk. I thought they might not let me go!'

'Excited?' she repeated and smiled. 'Then it's because of that.' She nodded up at the full moon and he frowned at her, not understanding. 'The full moon does that,' she told him. 'It makes men excited and angry and sleepless. It always has done and it always will.'

He thought about what she said unhappily. 'Is that not part of the old religion?'

She laughed, and it was like the merry laugh a child gives when she cartwheels through spring flowers. And in the end he had to smile himself, sheepishly.

'No, it is not,' she said, and sat so she could see him in the entrance to the cave. 'It is just one of the many strange things about the world. That is all. Not everything needs to be explained and understood.

83

That is what your monks want. They want to answer every question until there's nothing left.'

He thought about that and said nothing. He thought of the great debates he had left behind and he saw that in a way she was right. In a way.

'I don't think we want answers to everything,' and even as he spoke the words he noticed that he counted himself one of them. 'I think there is plenty we will never know and do not even try to explain.' Was that what he thought and what they also would have believed? He was not certain.

Her face smiled again as she looked at him. 'Everything you cannot explain you just call God!' she said. 'That is your easy way out!'

Now he wanted to creep back to his tower and his book and his inks, and say that all this talk had to do with the scholars. He was not one of them; he would copy their words but not join their arguments. He liked to be on the edge of the talk, to listen to two of them building and building their debate. It was like a game of invisible chess. But he had neither a head nor a heart for it himself, though he liked well enough to listen at the side in the shadows. And he admired them; perhaps he knew that now as he had not before. He had counted himself one of them.

'Do not look so anxious!' she said to him, and he turned back to her and smiled again. She made him think and that was good. She and her mother were outside their little world of the settlement and the chapels. Their world was not the only one and it was good for them to remember that.

'I brought you a gift,' she said gently. 'I thought of the work that you do and I wanted to make you something.' Now she looked away, shy, towards the silver-plated hills of the far island. Not a thing moved in the night; there was not the slightest noise. 'After the day I took you to the Well of the North Wind, my favourite place on the island, I did not know what to do. I know that I am ill and that I will die, but I do not know when. It is something I can do nothing about. And sometimes I am frightened and want to hide away, and sometimes I want only to live and laugh. That day I was afraid.'

Her eyes held him and he listened and tried to understand. 'Perhaps I will be like that again one day,' she said, 'but then perhaps you will remember. You will know it is the fear inside me.'

'I missed you when I did not see you,' he said. 'I wanted to come and find you but I did not have the courage. I thought you . . . I thought that I had said something that angered you. But you were often in my mind.'

He had never spoken such words before. He had never thought he would speak to her again. It was true that he had missed her, but he had also dared not think of her because he believed it was useless and impossible.

'So after that day,' she said, and now he saw the tiny vial in her hands, 'I went back on my own to the well, and I found special flowers. I made something for your hands and for the work they have to do.'

He looked at her, stunned. That she would do such a thing for him. Her eyes smiled. 'Give me your hands.'

He held them out, still speechless, and she let a few drops fall on his palms. Softly she smoothed them into his skin, and he caught the fragrance of it then, and it was so strong it all but left him dizzy. It was like the very scent of summer; it was as though she had found the summer and distilled it down to this. For him. She poured new drops now onto the tops of his hands and smoothed each finger in turn, and all at once he thought of that first day when he had met Colum, fearful and gauche and bewildered, and he had been told that his were the fourth pair of hands to work with the book. And he remembered too how they had taken him up into the tower and told him the sacred nature of his work, how he must always be careful with his hands.

'Will you draw something for me?' she asked suddenly, looking up.

'Now?' he said, surprised and foolish.

'No,' she said shyly, and looked back at his hands as still she worked with them. 'One day. One day, if it is possible.'

'Of course I will, Mara,' he said, and he wanted to kiss the top of her head as she bent over his hands but he did not. He turned his head slightly and put his left cheek there instead and closed his eyes. And she did not move.

*

Just days and days of stillness. The snow down on the islands; here and there almost to the very edge of the sea. Days of gathering driftwood and breaking the ice at the well for water. A cold that hurt like a wound in feet and hands. The waking in the middle of the night to hear the low voice of the wind, passing like a ghost from nowhere into nowhere. Days of hunger when there was all but nothing to eat, when even walking felt a penance and everywhere too far away. At midday the only sound ravens tumbling and talking their dark dialect in the white-blue silence of the sky. And yearning for the fire; hands yearning to be over the turf fire.

One day Larach came to find them. He was better, though his face was still hollow and the eyes staring from their caves. But he had learned to laugh again, even though the deaths he had left behind still haunted him.

He came to find them and they were silent as they waited, watching. Mostly they looked up as he came close, though one stared into the fire. He stood there and his shadow blocked the snowball sun from the open doorway. They looked, knowing he would speak, and waiting.

'Colum was weeping,' he said, his voice sore. 'He was only weeping.'

*

Had her oil made a difference in his hands or was it something else? He just knew he was on fire with pictures, and that he was drawing well. Somewhere very deep inside he was sure of it, though he would have said the words to no one in a thousand years. Yet he knew all the same; he was sure. That in itself brought him back to draw the more. It was like stoking a fire; once the first flames came you knew how to bring them on and wanted more. There were times he did not even want to sleep because he knew what lay in wait on the page; he could see it there, not yet drawn but sleeping. And though he dragged himself away, reluctant to sleep, he knew it was good to rest too. He came back restored, eye and hand steady. He knew the danger in going on just a little too long.

There was one morning he was down at the shore, by the little beach where he had shown the children his drawing. He was like a child himself; sure he was on his own and squatting there at the very edge of the tide, watching the ripples of clear water break over the sand. He was far away in himself.

'What is it that you want with my daughter?'

He gasped, all but toppled forwards in shock, and her hands reached out to steady his shoulders. But when she brought him back, she did not let him go. And her mouth again, rasping at his left ear: 'What is it that you want with my daughter?'

He knew who she was; there could be no doubt about that. It was her strength he remembered more than anything; a kind of strength he had scarcely known before. Not a mere physical might that gave a man the power to lift great rocks; it was more than that. A strength that went through her whole self; strength in her seeing, in her talking, in the way that she held things.

'I want to be her friend,' he found himself saying, and he had not spoken any words before that morning, so the shape of them felt strange in his mouth. 'I want to be good and kind. I mean no harm!'

Perhaps she relaxed her hold on him a fraction, but her voice was no less strong. 'You must know a little of what Mara has suffered, Fian. She has seen the face of death many times and come back. You must be careful with her. She is made of brittle things. And you could break her if you are not careful.'

Suddenly she swung Fian round so he faced her; spun him round so again he lost his balance and sat down awkwardly on the sand. He felt like a five-year-old child as he tried to hold her gaze.

All at once he seemed to waken from his inner cocoon and think straight, and he was back in his mind at the Well of the North Wind. 'I have been careful!' he said, and now he heard his heart's thud, and felt the blood rise in his face. 'It was Mara that . . .'

And then he stopped himself; he said no more. He could not betray her.

She looked at him and down at the sand between them. She took his two hands in her own and he did not try to take them back. 'I understand, Fian,' she said, and when he dared to gaze at her again her face was glassy. But she did not turn away. And it was strange how he felt strong as she held his hands. Something he had never known before that went through him and somehow made him strong too. He felt her strength.

'But you must know that she will die one day!' The words almost choked out of her, in grief and anger and pain.

'Maybe she can be healed.' The words burst out of him.

'No!' Sharp and taut, like the jerk of a rope. That was what he thought and she commanded stillness. She waited and the same power pulsed and pulsed through his hands. It was a strength that frightened him.

'There must be no false hope. You might offer that, you might even believe it. But Mara knows herself what will be, sooner or later. A long time ago she came to a place where she understood. And you must not take that away, with your promises and your prayers. If you will be a friend to her, if you will love her, you will not do that. Do you understand?'

The words almost shouted at him, but because of what was in her own heart. He knew that later, in the hours when he raked over every word.

'Yes, I understand and I promise,' he said, and his voice was soft and still he held her gaze. As the power came beat after beat through her hands.

Did she hold him then a moment before she got up and was gone? He could not remember, but at some point his hands were his own again and he had slumped to one side and realized that the water was lapping against his thigh. He looked up and there was no sign of her; it might have been that he had sat here always on his own and had done nothing more than imagine her presence. Yet he knew what had been all the same. He did not doubt that. And in the morning's blue wind there was the tanging of the bell, calling and calling them.

*

Fian found himself returning to the Well of the North Wind. Or at least he tried to find it. Before, he had just followed Mara and it had seemed easy, as though it was a straight path. There was a moment now he almost gave up in disgust and began tramping his way back. He tried to keep to higher ground, away from the deep slumps of bog, but he failed in that too. Once he had to climb out onto a rise on all fours and he felt cold and his pride hurt. He sat down at the top of the rise and had to admit that he was lost. Well, he would find his way back all right if he left while there was still plenty of light, but he felt he might have gone on wandering for many hours. All at once he smiled to himself at the foolishness of it; he smiled and he laughed. How long was it since last he had laughed? The truth was he couldn't remember, and now it felt good. Then he picked himself up because he was feeling the cold, and he decided he would give it one last try. If he failed he would admit defeat and turn back, no matter his hurt pride.

He fought again to keep high and quite suddenly he was out of the mire and into a tiny glen that led through beside high rocks to a view of the far sea. And he knew that he had been here that day with Mara, and he remembered the way from here. In a few minutes he found the place.

Before he sat down he crouched and looked at the pool of black water in the well. He would have passed it by had she not brought him here first and told him; it was no more than another bit of wetness in the moor. But he found his hand reaching out to cup some water and drink it. He swallowed a mouthful. It was warm; that was the first surprise. Not like the brisk flowing of river water in winter; this was still, held by the tight clasp of the grass and the heather. But clear and pure; he felt it deep inside. He wanted more. And he thought how the black surface was transformed to crystal clearness when he brought it up.

He sat a while and did nothing but watch. But for a few winter-pink clouds the sky was all but clear over the island, though a storm was coming in black chariots from the west. It was almost akin to an enormous flock of birds, or perhaps ten thousand flocks that flew together. And on the underside of these great black clouds were flutterings of lightning. At once he thought of the books of Daniel and Revelation; it was a manifestation of judgement that drove over the sea towards him. And for a moment, for a second, that was a thought that came to him. This was the judgement.

*

'Colum wants you to come to speak with him. Tonight.'

Neil had come up the stairs that morning to find him. Fian had turned around to look at him, the edge of a smile on his face, for Neil was the greatest among them for tricks. It was hard to know when he was deadly serious and when fooling, and Fian had fallen into too many of his traps. But there was no cruelty in him; he was kindness itself to little Cuillin, would stop and talk to him at the garden, make sure he was never forgotten.

'As sure as I am that the sun will rise tomorrow, Colum wants to see you tonight. The day will come when no one believes a thing I say . . .'

He was already on his way down the staircase and Fian called after him: 'We would not have you any different, Neil. Do not despair of us . . .'

He was rather excited that Colum wanted to see him. He thought of what it could be as he went back to his page. They did not see Colum so much now; often he retreated to his cell and did not want to be disturbed. Better not bring the bear from hibernation: that was how Cuan had put it one day when the bear had been all claws with him. But they saw well enough how he wrestled with growing old. He fought against his weaknesses and they wept for him. He wanted to admit nothing and be the master he once had been. The man inside had the spirit still of a bear; it was just that on the outside the bear was failing. Yet somehow the older he became the more they loved him. Rare was it that a word was spoken against him, and woe betide any man who spoke ill of him without due thought.

And so Fian went with a light heart. He remembered the first time he met Colum and how everything in him shook. Perhaps there was something of the leader in him that liked that, that had not wanted to dispel it completely when he had chased Fian off to find Ruach. He had come away half-sick with fear, his head a bewilderment of new names and places.

'So tell me how the book is progressing!'

The grey-blue eyes flashed at him, listening intently and excited. Every third breath or so he drew in more air as though he was always searching a bit more now, yet he followed every word. And Fian poured out what he had done, not as a pupil who needs the praise of a teacher, but as one lover of words to another. Not boastful, only glad for what had been found, like one who had searched for gold in a river.

'Fian, there is somewhere I want you to go.'

As he spoke the words Colum got up and turned away, moved about in the shadows. They were well enough used to it; tired he might be, but he could never stay still for long. It was as though he thought better on his feet.

'It is a listening place. This is a doing place, unless you are like Ruach and hide away among green stones. But there are times for listening, too, and that is what I want you to do now. It is another island, but a very different kind of place.'

They looked at each other in the light now; the one man standing and the other seated. Fian was trying to think about his words; this was not what he had expected. He did not know if it was a gift or a punishment. Nor did he rightly know what questions to ask. There was silence for a moment and the eyes searched each other.

'I am . . . I am in the middle of so much,' Fian said. 'When can I come back? How long must I stay away? I don't understand why it should be now!'

'Sometimes it is good to let the well fill with water,' said Colum, and at once Fian thought of the well he had come to know, and he saw Mara's face and he tasted again the deep purity of that water.

Fian dared to answer, though he knew well that he must be careful. 'There is water, though, and in abundance. I am working as I have never done before and I am loath to leave.' His voice was soft.

'Beware when there seems to be so much water to draw!' said Colum, and he sat once more and leaned close to Fian. There was the big breath, and the grey-blue eyes flickered in the light. Fian tried to read them, to know what was behind them. He had to tread carefully or the bear would be there and the saint no more.

'Then is it never possible to be content with what one has? Does one always have to be wary, whether there is too little or too much? You told me there would be days here when I wanted to be away, when I had had enough and could stomach no more. I have struggled and yet now I have found. I do not want to leave when I am finding.'

For a second he thought the bear was going to rise and pounce. Then the big breath and the eyes searched and thought and then returned. 'I am not asking you, Fian,' he said, and the voice was calm but sure. Fian moved where he sat and made as though to speak again.

'And one more thing,' Colum said. 'I want there to be no goodbyes.'

*

Even before dawn the boat, and a cold the like of which he had never known. Perhaps because of the wind on the water, and the pain of it on his face, making his eyes run with water. And those tears seemed to freeze on his cheeks and on the bones above his cheeks, and he bent his head and closed his eyes for he could hardly bear the soreness.

It would be a beautiful morning and he could see none of it. He did not understand and in the one moment when he had courage enough to lift his head he saw the tower and his heart flamed with the thought of the book. He thought of it now as his book, and he could not bear the idea of another hand working on its words. And yet that must have been the way of it with the three who came before. Strange to think he still did not know what had become of them and had never asked. Perhaps the truth was that he did not want or need to know.

He half curled in the bottom of the boat to be out of the flensing of the wind. He knew nothing: where he was going, how far away it might be, how long he was to be there. And yet he did know it was hardly unusual. Men like Larach would have wanted nothing less. Was it that he had been spoiled too long? Was that what it was?

His companion in the boat, the man who now took him away, said not a word. He was the master of the vessel and nothing more. His eyes took in the water, the rocks, the sky. Twice Fian thought of asking him where they were going, and twice he shut his mouth once more.

All at once he did look up and he saw away over to one side a stony beach. It was at once familiar yet it took a moment to know why.

He was seeing it the wrong way round. But the great rock that lay behind and something about the line of the shore; he was sure he recognized both. Then he knew and would almost have smiled had the wind not come again and the tears begun to flow from his eyes so he had to hide his head once more. Of course, it was Colum's beach, the place where once he had landed. And the place where Ruach hid to search for his beloved green stones.

It was a tiny comfort to see the place. And yet now as they went further and further away from the island, he realized how he had come to love it. Larach had said something about that, about returning to the island after all the hardship they had known in the empty, barren landfalls of the north. It was only when you could come back and *know* just how precious it always had been.

Now he saw the island for the last time. They were turning round a headland to the south and in a moment it would be swallowed and lost. His eyes smarted and he felt a fool, but he could not help it. He thought of them waking in the dwelling and finding him gone; he heard in his head their puzzled questions. What Neil would say of the work-hungry scribe. He saw them all and he loved them.

Even now, on this perfect winter morning, there was a swell to the water and a faint sickness rose within him. They were turning round the headland and riding the waves. He crouched down in the boat once more and knew he was no good sailor. Larach and his companions would have thrown him overboard for his uselessness. And he felt that now; he felt helpless and hopeless. The only good in him was left behind in the tower on the island, and that was the truth.

*

He woke when the boat thudded against rocks. He did not want even to raise his head for he had felt so sick the last hours. He had curled to sleep in the bottom of the boat and now he dragged himself up and reached out a hand for the bundle of things he had brought with him. The man shoved him roughly onto the shore.

'Tell Goloch I will be back for you when I am told!'

Fian could barely remember his own name let alone the complexity of such a message. He nodded and turned away, and sank down pathetically among the stones. His eyes ranged over them and he saw that they were all the same – thin flakes of stone the like of which he had never seen before. The sky and the sea and the rocks swam together and he was sick. By the time he looked up again the boat had long since vanished.

There was a rough stone staircase leading up from the landing place, and it was built of the same thin, grey slices of stone he had seen on the shore. He felt well enough to stand tall and look about him. It was the greyest place he had seen in all his life. A hump-backed rock; that was effectively what it was, and up above him he now saw three or four shelters that were made out of the grey stone. From where he stood they might have been the humps of mythical creatures. He saw their doorways and slits of windows. Fian was so weak he could only climb the staircase bit by bit. He had to lean and rest sometimes, and then he looked back over the sea, at the island hills and their shoulders of snow. They were so bright with sun he could hardly look at them, but the place to which he had been brought was shrouded in shadow. He thought with bitter irony that this was what purgatory must be like.

By the time he reached the dwellings he was hungry. There was no one there. They stood in silence, ghostly and empty. They had been built under the ridge of what he assumed was an island; they might be in near permanent shadow, but at least they were protected from the wind. Fian crouched and waited, and in the end he lay down and went to sleep.

When he woke again, after what might have been one hour or ten, he found himself inside one of the stone shelters. He had a woollen blanket over him and when he sat up he saw that there was a cup beside him and a little stack of fragments of oatcake. He ate hungrily and drank. The water was good, partly because he had drunk nothing now for a long time – yet it was more than that. With a stab he thought of the water of the Well of the North Wind and its clarity and purity, the way it reached to the very roots when one drank. And then a face appeared in the doorway. It was that of a young boy. He had a great tumble of thick ginger curls and freckled cheeks. The blue eyes glittered over Fian, friendly and alive.

'My name is Goloch,' he said. 'Are you feeling better?'

Fian nodded and reached for the cup to ask for more water.

'Most people who come here are sick when they arrive. It's the last bit of the crossing; you might as well be on the back of a horse, even on a calm day like this. But there's no one else here at the moment. From tomorrow I'll leave you in silence because that was what I was told to do, but I'll always be here if you need me. Later I can show you the island if you want. But sleep a while and I'll bring you more water.'

The boy had gone before Fian could say thank you. The kindness touched him nonetheless, perhaps all the more because of the way he had had to leave that morning, because of his sickness and the grey stone. When the boy came back and reached in with the cup, he thanked him from the heart.

Later they crossed the island. Goloch was ten paces ahead of him, talking all the time and telling him about the landing place, the great whirlpool to the south, the ones who had first come from Ireland and who lived west of here, where he himself had come from, and a whole host of other things ranging from sea monsters to the making of oatcakes.

Fian wondered if monks came here prepared for silence or chose rather to flee into it, but he was glad of Goloch's company all the same. For his part the boy was not the least interested in Fian's provenance, and Fian was glad enough to do little more than listen. He let some of the talk wash over him, nodding when he thought it appropriate, and he realized that it was a very long time since he had heard anyone talk so much. Perhaps on a wet day when there had been yet another argument about angels in the dwelling, and several of the young scribes had come and joined in too. But most often Fian had fled then, back to the quiet dark of the tower.

There was nowhere beautiful on the island, but then perhaps that was why it had been chosen. There were no trees; almost nothing green at all. It was most certainly a desert place, the sort of escape that Larach and his kind yearned for. That he could understand well enough, but it was when they came back bragging about the austerity and how many days they had managed to endure . . .

But why had Colum sent him now? It was true enough he had been nowhere else for long enough, but then he was not fully one of them. He was on the fringes of their world and content to be so, neither completely believing nor fully doubting, bound to them and yet not. He wondered if that was the reason, to break him in like a wild horse through solitude and hunger and greyness. To let God shatter at last the safe walls he had built up around himself.

Now, that day, he fed Goloch sprats of questions and half listened to the answers. The boy made a fire and something warm out of oatmeal that Fian hoped he would never have to eat again. The sky turned a deep blue and Fian thought of the songs and the music there could have been around such a fire. How many times had he slipped away from such gatherings?

There he goes! Back to his book, boys, and he even hangs his head in shame! He heard Neil's voice, joyous and full of good-heartedness, and he made himself listen to Goloch and his stories. It was all he could do.

In the end he could listen no more, and he thanked Goloch for looking after him well. He made to leave for the well and a last drink of water.

'Pay heed to your dreams!' the boy called after him. 'Everyone who comes here dreams!'

*

It was the very dead of night and all the settlement slept. The last argument had been left in laughter and half-hugged shoulders. No lights shone. About midnight there was a crystalling of snow and then nothing, not so much as a breath of wind. The only sound came from Colum's chamber, much later, and by then he was ragged and the bear in him close to breaking loose.

'I have done what you bid me and I can do no more, so let that be an end of it! No, I will not talk about it, nor will I do so tomorrow! I am troubled by what I have done and would that I were not. He is gone and that is what you wanted.'

Still the other voice spoke in the shadows and would not be done. He breathed and kept the bear on its chain; his voice was small but dangerous.

'It is the middle of the night and I am an old man. I should not be here and would that I were not. There are times I grow tired of what I carry and this is one of those times. So leave me and let us pray that what we have done – yes, what I have done and what you have done – may be for the best. I bid you goodnight and I ask that you leave me in peace.'

The shadow went; hurried out into the hugeness of the night. And Colum closed his eyes at last, though his heart did not rest. Sometimes he yearned for an earthly master to give him counsel. The world came to him and wanted answers; to whom was *he* to turn? There were times when God was silent. Perhaps now, after all these years, even more silent. He did not know if he believed all the words he had spoken to Fian, and that troubled him. He wanted to believe them and yet he was not certain. For whom had he spoken them? For Fian, for himself, or for his visitor?

At the south end of the island Ruach kept his vigil. He had vowed he would sleep when the last piece of wood was burned, but he kept going to find more. He was too frightened of what he might find in his dreams. Still nothing was clear; only a shadow moved on the edge of his consciousness and troubled him. He worried for Fian and did not know why. An otter came out of the shadows and melted into the water without a thought. If only he might possess such courage; to enter the darkness with the whole of his heart.

*

It is strange how we are not missed. All of us want to be, especially when we are dead and have departed for good, yet then we cannot know how we have been missed. But we want to return and know that somehow our not being in the familiar place made a difference. That the days were different for those we left behind.

Perhaps it was as much because Fian was so often up in the tower that his absence was barely noted that first day. There was bread to be made. A group had stayed up late the night before talking to Larach; he had assumed something of the mantle of the hero since he recovered. A number of the young men had grown fascinated by the dream of desert places, and he had found one and endured there and returned. Perhaps his gaunt face and hollow cheeks made his status all the more heroic. Perhaps he limped on that left leg just a little more when he knew they were watching. So Fian's empty bed was hardly noticed until the next evening. Even then, though it was talked about, there was little concern. He might be working on a new page – and they knew that of late there had been plenty. Or he might have gone to find Ruach. They knew well enough that the settlement could be too much for Fian too; the endless babble of the scribes and their thirst for answers. He was one of them and yet he was not. They accepted him and did not need to understand him.

It was only on the following day that they first began to puzzle over his absence. Neil went up to the tower, taking the steps two at a time and humming something that he himself had composed only a few days before. He stopped abruptly, seeing at once the place was empty. He had been all but certain he would find the artist here, his head bent over the page. And he had not been here for long enough. Neil stood there a second, waiting and thinking. Then where could he be?

In the end it was Colum himself who told them, and though they were a moment surprised, they quickly forgot to be. And the place where Fian always was simply filled. He was not missed. Cuan and Neil spoke of him once or twice in the first days, but not thereafter.

Only Ruach remembered him, where he kept his silent vigil down at the south end of the island. Sometimes he did no more than sit at the mouth of the overhang where he sheltered, huddled in to himself and looking out always onto the sea. He did not even have the desire to search for stones.

And the girl remembered him. She knew that he had gone and she felt his absence somewhere deep inside. She went across the moors to the Well of the North Wind, slow and limping, wishing he was with her, and wishing it was not winter and that there might be flowers to gather, for that would have been a comfort. But she did not know why it was that he had gone.

*

Strange that the last thing of which Goloch had spoken was dreams, for Fian had no sense of dreaming that first night. He had no sense of sleeping deeply, for he lay on almost pure rock, and he turned and turned again. But it was as though he flowed always through strange water, until at last he lay a long time and knew that it was morning.

He knew where he was as soon as he opened his eyes. The light came from a hundred places in the stone beehive in which he lay. There was no sound – of water, of wind, of anything. It was seldom he woke to silence. No matter the earliness of the hour there would be talking close by; some huddle of scholars who had slept a couple of hours and had returned now to the tussles of the night before. Or talk about the bringing in of a boat or the mending of a wall, at the same time as a debate over some phrase of music. Talk was part of the fabric of their garments.

And so the absence of it was strange. He felt lonely for the first time since childhood, since his mother chased him out and he went down to draw in the sand. That was why he had begun to draw. Yet he could not even do that here, he thought, as he went out at last into the cold grey wretchedness of the morning. Every beach was made of stone. It was as though this place had been chosen for him as somewhere he could not hide. There was nowhere to escape from himself.

He drank a long time. He crouched by the well and looked all around. The evening before there had been shimmerings of islands to the south; now the mist had swallowed them. He could not even see the place where water met sky; they were as one. Even the sea did not move but came and lipped the island shore without a sound.

He walked the circumference of the island and was almost glad of the noise his feet made on the stones. All he found on the far side was a gully that went straight down from the top of the island to the shore. It was as though lightning had once struck it and burned a mark there for ever. But there was nothing to find except a rubble of broken stones.

He went back to his cell because there seemed nowhere else to go. Inside was a new stack of pieces of oatcake. It was apparent that Goloch knew his task well: to be invisible but to watch those who came here without fail.

It suddenly struck him that this was a place Mara would not like either, for there were no flowers. The thought of her was like a shock of light. And yet it came to him at that moment, too, that he barely knew her. There was far more that he did not know than he knew. There had been too little time; nothing like enough!

And when he thought of Mara he remembered her mother also, and the morning she had found him at the tide's edge and held him. It was as though she had put a knife to his throat. She had wanted no talk of her daughter's healing and yet why should there not be? Why could the God they believed in not take away her sickness?

He looked up at the pieces of light that showed between the stones. He did not know what to pray for himself and Colum had wanted him to come to pray. So if he could not pray for himself, he would pray for Mara.

*

Ruach saw a storm coming, but he did not know if it was a real storm or one of anger and strife. He fretted because the shadow would not come closer; he felt it on the edge of everything. He could not walk over the beach without seeing it there ahead of him, and at night he was afraid of closing his eyes. For all that, he would rather be where he was. He could not have borne the talk and argument and laughter of the settlement; he could not have answered questions about the setting of fires or the fetching of water. He knew that he was only a stone's throw from escaping into his own death. His existence was bearable because shadows came, most often in dreams, and a few days later they manifested themselves, he understood them, and the storm broke. The day that followed a storm was nothing less than blessed release. He felt whole and unafraid; he could laugh and hear song, talk and forget himself. He could love and feel loved.

But never had a storm lasted so long. Never had a shadow lingered at the edge of his consciousness like this without coming alive. All he knew, or thought he knew, was that it had something to do with Fian. But there was little help in that. It was insufficient; a fragment of possibility with which he could do nothing. And so he gathered wood and fed a fire; he wandered over the green glens at the island's south end finding the leaves of a sour herb he could eat, and drinking water from a loud stream that snaked from the high ground.

Nothing. Just the sea's breathing; its suck and fall, suck and fall. There were mornings when he felt stronger, after he had slept a few hours of the darkness away. Then he clattered down over the rocks to the tide's edge and was a child again, crouching in search of fragments of translucent green stone. He searched for a perfect one; an oval stone the size perhaps of his thumbnail. When it rolled in his palm it would be dark, almost black, but when held against the light it would turn lemon yellow, a little world of caverns and ledges. He would play his game with the sea; hunching as close to the waves as he dared, before skipping back as the next wall of thunder rolled in. But more often as the morning progressed he sat somewhere higher up, close to the overhang where he had his fire and curled to sleep, to sit and sift. Perhaps it was the sheer rhythm of his hands that comforted; the sifting and sifting of little hills of shingle. It was like the rhythm of the sea, the in-breath and the out-breath. But by the afternoon he could do nothing. Often he could not walk as far as the tide's edge. The fear had descended and he almost saw the shadow there on the horizon, on the edge of the outer world and of the inner one also. He tried to pray and most often his prayers were like flimsy things of grass that blew away on the wind. He just crouched and rocked, backwards and forwards, and sometimes he cried. There were flickerings of home and growing up; he remembered a wide, green place and the soft voice of his mother. She rocked him and sang a song that was to send him to sleep, but he fought against sleeping because he liked the song too much.

It was when the dark began to descend that he felt most afraid. Now it was almost midwinter and the shortest days of the year. Sometimes he managed to struggle up to the summit of one of the little hills to watch the sun's fall. He kept the light to the last, then crept back down through the shadows that were growing already to hide in his cave. His fire was tiny and he fed it fragments; it was there he kept watch as the sea boomed around him invisible in the darkness. He could not pray but he sang; that is, he sang inside. He heard slow and beautiful psalms sung in his head; he heard them sometimes over and over again, and they kept the shadow from falling across him completely.

But often the night was all but over by the time he slept. It would have been so easy to get up and wade into the sea. All of this would be over; there would be no more waiting. No more nights like this. Sometimes, just sometimes, sleep came over him as he lay huddled there under the rocks. He woke in the light of a new day, rejoicing that he had slept at all.

The night after Fian left he did not sleep. The dawn came, grey and cold, like a wolf. The shadow had not left him; all night it had been there, closer yet still invisible. His hands and feet hurt so much he cried. He knew that he had to move. He knew, too, that he could not do this much longer. And then the words came to him: *he must go to speak with Colum*. He let them echo in his head before he truly understood them. Yes, it was all that he had left. Even then, he got up and dragged himself over the top of the shore. The world was wrapped in wool. He started walking.

*

Goloch crouched in the doorway. The silhouette of him, the wild curls trailing over his neck and shoulders. He did not come in to the cell. 'I forgot to take you to the chapel,' he said. 'You were sick when you arrived, and then you had to have food, and when I showed you everywhere else I didn't take you there. I'm sorry to have broken your silence.'

Fian was not in the least sorry, but he was amused that Goloch had to break it with quite so many words. It was obvious he was waiting. 'Well, will you take me there?' Fian asked.

They walked out past the well and down to the end of the island. Fian had a sense of it now; it was a long, thin tapering shape – pointed at both ends and with one single ridge of hill along its middle. The gully ran down from hill to sea on one side.

When they reached the end of the island (what somehow Fian felt must be the south), Goloch began clambering up towards the top. There was rubble everywhere; piles and piles of the strange grey shards. Sometimes he went on all fours because of the slithering piles of them and the steepness of the slope. But he was younger and fitter than Fian who came tottering behind him, clutching strands of grass whenever he found them. He had spent too long in the tower with his book.

Close to the top Goloch turned to watch how he was getting on and to wait for him. And as he straightened up Fian saw there was something he had not noticed before; a hole that looked as though it had been carved out of the very hillside. Goloch waited until Fian had caught up with him and recovered his breath. Then he disappeared into darkness.

The chamber was about six or ten feet deep. It took a moment for Fian to see anything at all, but vague shapes began to grow out of the gloom. Something that might have been a font; ledges in the walls for candles; smooth surfaces for seats.

'No one knows if it was carved like this or if it's an accident of creation,' said Goloch. He shrugged his shoulders and smiled, looked about him at the ceiling and the walls. 'And what does it matter! But the legend is that it was a hiding place, that it was made by God for someone in great need. That is why the island was seen as holy in the beginning. There are many years of prayer in this place.'

Fian nodded. Above all, it was an escape from the greyness, a greyness he thought might have driven him mad in the end. He thanked Goloch as the rock chapel came alive moment by moment. The boy went in the end, though it was clear he had no wish to go. And Fian wished that he could have brought Mara here. He remembered the cave where they had crouched in the moonlight and where she had taken and anointed his hands with the oil she had made for them. And he prayed for her and prayed for her; just the same words over and over in his head. He prayed that she might be kept safe and well.

*

Colum gave Ruach wine (watered down, for he saw how weak he was, and how his hands shook). He put some knots of bog oak on the fire and he brought Ruach close in to the flames and wrapped a blanket around the remains of his shoulders. In all the years he had not seen him like this.

'Have you eaten, Ruach? You cannot live down there on nothing! You must come back and let us care for you for a time! There will be space in the infirmary and you can sleep. Your eyes tell me you have not slept for days!'

'I am haunted by a shadow.' The voice little more than a whisper, and Colum took his hands and chafed them, for they were like stone with cold. Ruach stared into the flames and his eyes glistened with light. 'That is why I came back,' he went on, and each word was like a painful step. 'I long for release and there is none. The shadow is out there and will not come close. I cannot sleep for fear of it.'

'Then I will pray with you and we will ask that you are able to see and that this can be at an end!' said Colum, and he held an open hand under Ruach's chin and tilted the cup to his lips. As he did so he saw the blood around Ruach's pupils and how his eyes wandered. Like a man who has fled a war, he realized. This must not go on.

He was about to ask more and thought better of it. Ruach was half mad with hunger and thirst and exhaustion; he stood on the cliff edge of delirium. He must be brought back first; that was the only hope.

Three times others knocked on the door asking to see Colum, and three times he sent them scuttling. He had neglected Ruach and he knew it. This man who had been troubled all his days by ghosts and dreams, yet who never faltered in his trust. In the days of Rome they could have set him against lions and gladiators; Ruach would have gone out ready, his life held in his open hands. There were younger, stronger voices here now; perhaps they were heard too often and the Ruachs were left in the shadows. Yet it did not help that more of his days were spent hidden in a cave than here in the settlement; there was little Colum could do for him there. Maybe now was the time to bring him back among them . . .

He made up a little gruel in a bowl and fed it to him. Already Ruach was stronger; his hands had steadied and there was colour in his face. Still he stared into the fire, but there was less madness in those eyes. As Colum fed him he prayed in the silence of his heart, over and over again.

'Do you have any clue?' he asked softly. 'Have you any thought of what the darkness might be, Ruach? Tell me if you have had so much as a glimpse.'

113

And Ruach turned. There was a crumb of gruel on his upper lip as he lifted his face and Colum drew back, the empty bowl held in his hands. 'Fian,' he said, without a moment's hesitation, and it was as though he breathed his name rather than spoke it. 'I am anxious for Fian, that is all I know. There is more, and that I cannot find, but I am anxious for Fian!'

Colum got up and moved away, the bowl in his hands. He felt Ruach's eyes watching him, even as he turned away. Finally he put down the bowl. 'Fian?' he said, his voice a question. 'You are sure that it is Fian you have seen?'

He came back at last, the cup full of more wine and water for Ruach.

'Yes, it is. Over and over again. Yet it is only a part of what I am looking for. That I know too. Why is it that I should be anxious for him? When he is only working on the book!'

'He is over on the little island for a time of quiet. Come now, Ruach, take some more wine and let your strength recover! How many days is it since you ate and drank as you should have done? Come, let me pour some!'

But Ruach held his arm away. His eyes were thinking, slowly. 'On the island? He has never been there before. Did Fian choose to go himself?' There was surprise, puzzlement, in his voice.

'He is there and he is safe!' Colum said, and again he tried to hold the cup to Ruach's lips. But Ruach was still thinking and wondering, still not able to understand. For every question there had to be another.

'Has something happened to him?' asked Ruach.

*

He thought of all he did not know about her. If they had come to the island from somewhere else. Where her mother especially had come from, and how she had learned to heal. Where her brother was now. How they had first known about flowers and which ones to pick. What they thought of Colum. What the others on the island thought. There was much more about her that he did not know than he knew. And yet what he did know was that he missed her, more than anyone before in his life. Perhaps it was as much for that very reason; he did not know her well enough and he yearned to know her better. It felt as though he had been imprisoned here against his will and that with every day that passed he missed her more and wanted to go back the more. And it multiplied in his head because there was no news. The water was silent and there was nothing, day after day.

He thought he might have gone mad had he not had the chapel to visit. He wanted to pray there, but his prayers were ragged things that seemed to fall to nothing. The harder he tried, the more he felt the wretchedness of his inadequacy. He remembered that Neil had once clapped him on the shoulder and said that God accepted those who prayed with pen and ink. But he felt all the same that it was second best, and that they considered it so. He had gone on comforting himself with the thought that he *did* pray with pen and ink, but now that his hands were empty . . .

His thoughts flickered. All at once he would see Mara in his mind's eye out with her basket on the moorland. He would begin to imagine his conversation with her; a conversation they had never had. It was as though he woke up with guilt, knowing that his prayer had strayed. Yet did God require long and torn-out implorings? Did that make him listen more than to a moment's prayer from the heart? Was it that we made God man by imagining our prayers must be like the hammerings on a locked door? Or was that simply the excuse we had created for ourselves?

At least he felt secure in the chapel. He liked it best on days of storm, for he was sheltered and looked out from a window onto the world. He crouched dry and warm within; a lit candle fluttered on the shelf above him. He prayed in pieces. That was what he decided in the end. He prayed in pieces.

*

It was Mara's mother who brought the light on the first day of the new year. Wind-still it was; nothing moved, perhaps in all the world. And the furthest hills cut out of sharpness, their sides that were pure with snow catching the sun's fire. The sea like glass; one single mirror of white-blue in every direction one looked. And it was not cold; here in the shelter of the settlement it was not a winter's day. When Larach went to pray in the hour before dawn he stood still a long time and listened to his own breathing and the tiny sounds of birds somewhere close by. He remembered the island in the

116

north, and a morning it had been little different from this, and he thought of the three friends he had lost and he bowed his head. So in the hour that he prayed, the sun rose over the far island, and its path over the sea was unbroken.

It was Mara's mother who brought the light. She held it safe in a stone bowl, and her hands shielded the flame. They waited for her up at the settlement; the scribes and the sculptors, the musicians and the scholars – they stood together at the edge of the path that led to the chapels and they watched her walking. They were all silent; for once there was not so much as a word between them. They stood at a strange gateway and were content with silence, and through them – in a thousand different ways – poured the memories of the days of the year that had been.

Even Ruach stood among them, stooped and older, yet a pale light back in his face and his eyes no longer bloodshot. They had given him something that made him sleep for two nights and two days, dreamless. The shadow had neither gone nor come closer; it waited and would not show its face, but Ruach had stayed with them all the same. He had found solace in the songs, especially late at night when he was most troubled. And they were good to him; they knew what he carried and they held little edges of the weight, to let his walk be lighter. He watched the light coming now, slow and steady, and it was beautiful. And at last Colum took the living light from her; an old light for a new year. And Colum prayed aloud, and it was so still he did not need to raise his voice and every one of them heard him well. And Ruach thought there was a skylark above his head as he prayed, twirling in the blue sky and singing. There was none, but there might have been.

117

So Mara's mother stood with them too and heard Colum's prayer. But her daughter was not with her.

*

Fian wrote in the sand. He wrote strange things he had never imagined before and they came alive and turned in the air and roared at him as they flew away. He fell backwards into the sand and cried, but his cry was soundless, and then he saw his mother at the top of the steep slope. She was shouting at him but he could not hear her words. His brothers rushed down the slope towards him and swept him off his feet. He landed in the water on his back and the cold tore him. But it was not day now, it was night, and he saw the stars bright and crackling in the blue skies. He stretched his hand up from the water and could draw in the dark skies.

It was like that Goloch found him in the cell. His forehead hot and wet with fever, locked in a strange tossing of nightmare. Goloch brought water from the well and made him drink; he brought him up from where he lay shivering on the stony ground and trickled crystal water into him. Some of it ran down the sides of Fian's mouth, but it did not matter. A little was not lost. Goloch came with his own blankets and wrapped Fian's quivering fever. A whole night he stayed with him, not sleeping, but watching and watching, listening to the breathing that raged and was not itself, leaving him only to get more water from the well.

She wanted to take him somewhere and he said that he would go. He carried the basket because of her limp and she led him. He did not know where it was and the hill became steeper and steeper until it was a cliff edge. But she kept on calling him and telling him to follow because there would be flowers there. And he could see them. On the tiniest ledge of rock at the very top were the brightest and the best. And in his head he knew that this was martyrdom; that was the reason they were so good and beautiful. But he did not know if they were real or a metaphor, he only knew that he had to paint them. Yet how could he when there was nothing to paint with? And what mattered more than anything was that Mara did not fall. He had to stop her from falling; that he knew with all his heart and soul, and he held her as she struggled on the cliff edge. He held her firm and must not let her fall.

*

'Where is Fian, Mother?'

'Sleep, child, you know that you must sleep! You woke because of the storm and now you must go back to sleep. Let me wrap you in the blanket, and let me put a couple of drops of the most healing flower on it. For you must get better; you must be well; you must worry for nothing!'

And it was as though Mara was sinking through her bed into another place. She knew somewhere what it was that she wanted to ask her mother, but the words were like fragments of wood on a shore. They were brittle and they broke as she tried to hold them, and she could not put them back together. She saw Fian in front of her yet he had changed and she did not know how. It was him and yet not. She called out to him with all the strength that was in her but although he saw her he was far away. All that remained was his name; that was the only word that was intact and she kept it and repeated it over and over as she sank down into the darkness. It was no longer her bed, it was the moorland; it was the black turf of the moorland and she was as a flower pressed beneath its weight, deeper and deeper.

*

In the middle of the night Ruach broke into Colum's cell; he did not even knock on the door but broke through it. Weakened though he was from his sleepless days of hunger at the south end, he possessed a strength that came from beyond him, for now he had seen. That night he had seen and known, and now there was not a moment to be lost.

'Waken up, master! Waken up!'

He rolled Colum in his bed as a small child might roll a younger sibling, foolishly and mercilessly, repeating the same words over and over again. Colum rose up in the bed and hauled Ruach away from him, not knowing who or what he was in the blackness. No one had roused him like that since the days of his childhood in Ireland, and they knew better than to drag him from sleep! Old as he was he was strong, and he knocked Ruach to the floor as if he had been little more than a doll. Then at last he had a candle lit and the two faces were yellow in its flutter. Both of them gasping for breath.

'What is the meaning of this?' Every one of Colum's words was a rock and full of weight. Ruach crouched by the bed, trembling, but what he carried with him was bigger than his fear of Colum.

'I have seen,' he said. 'I have seen that Fian is sick, sick unto death. The shadow has broken and I know. There is something more that I cannot find, but that much is certain. He must be brought back; he must be brought back in time, I beseech you!'

And again like a child, like a child that must have its way at whatever cost, he hurled himself at Colum and began shaking him. Colum tossed him to the floor as a bear might brush aside a butterfly, but he would have no more of this. When Ruach picked himself up, more hurt inside than out, he could hear what his master's eyes said. He needed no translation and Colum held him in his gaze until he was ready.

'I have heard you, Ruach, and at first light I will start to find him. I can do nothing in the pitch dark. Let that be my word!'

And Ruach went out unsteadily, like a drunk man, into the cloister. He crouched there a time, breathing, and he heard something, very far away. It was like wolves; the rising of the voices of wolves. He listened and did not know how long he crouched there. Still they rose and still he did not know what it was, almost like one of his dreams. And then all at once it broke through to him: it was the wind, the rising of the wind.

*

All of those days Fian did not dream. He wandered in half-awake nightmare, where Goloch's face swam before his and the boy spoke to him, but he could not understand what he was saying. That was when the fever had come upon him, but before that he remembered

121

nothing; he woke in the morning with not a flicker of a memory of a single dream. In those days before the fever that surprised him, he woke always puzzled that he remembered nothing, for it had been Goloch himself that warned him of them on the very first night.

Now Goloch was afraid that he would die under the fever. He did not know what to do; he had to sit and watch over Fian as he gabbled and shouted in his wanderings – above all he had to make sure that he drank. But how could he leave him to go for help? There was no one else on the island and he had no way of summoning help without leaving. He had prayed the calm might last, that the day would come when Fian was well enough for him to leave so he might send for help. But the fever rose and fell; as soon as he hoped it was lessening a new night came and the raging was as bad as it had been. Then, when the weather had held and held, it suddenly broke. Like a wild horse that has escaped from the reins that have kept it, the wind rose and went mad. Goloch even feared one night that the beehive cell where he slept beside Fian might fall in with the strength of it. In his heart he knew it would not; the hands that built it knew their work. And not a single one of the stones so much as moved.

But now he truly feared. Fian was as sick as ever, and there was little chance of the boatman Oran braving these seas now to take him back to the monastery. There was frail hope of Goloch getting word to Oran to begin with. The boy was brave, but there was one night he sat cross-legged in the beehive cell and wept, for he did not know what was left to do. And his own prayers were dry and useless.

It was then that Ruach came to Fian in dream. There was no let-up in the savagery of the wind and waves, yet there was a time of calm in the fever. The incomprehensible babble of his delirium stilled and he slept. Goloch even had to hold the back of his hand before Fian's nose and mouth to make certain he still breathed. But he did.

Ruach came towards him in dream. Ruach, not anguished and distraught, but clear-eyed and well. He came as though stooping forwards to look at Fian, as though he knew his sickness and saw it. He was speaking, though Fian could not make out what he said, and the words were not addressed to him. Ruach came close and looked at him, searched his face so clearly that Fian could see the bloodshot eyes and how they moved as they searched him. How long it lasted he did not know; it was timeless, as all things are in the world of dreams. But it happened.

*

The bell tanged and tanged in the January sky, but its note was blown into nowhere. Somehow it was a living metaphor on this day. All of them gathered from the storm; it was more that they were blown together, for now they knew that it was winter. Now they were paying for the weeks of calm.

And all talk and laughter was blown away too; it was as though nothing remained but knuckled hands and bewildered eyes. For this death they did not understand; this death they had not known would be.

It was Colum that spoke. Two days before he would have been too weak, he could not have stood – but he was determined. It was

123

like blowing the amber embers of a turf fire, hour after hour and refusing to give up hope, and the flame beginning again at last. But they did not all hear him; as the bell had been, so was his voice blown away by the wind and he did not have the strength to drown it out. Neil saw his face and the huge sadness that was in it; the blue eyes that spoke their sorrow.

He stood and did not hide the stick he leaned on. He spoke and Neil wondered what else it was he heard in Colum's voice, for there was of a certainty something he did not recognize and had not heard before. But he could not find what it was.

And then, when Colum had finished at last, the whole island started out onto the moorland, for that was where the grave was to be. There had been no question about that. Some of the young boys, scholars and scribes, had hacked and chipped at the chosen place for the best part of the day. Soft the ground might be, but it was a knot-work of roots and cluttered with lumps of stone. The boys came back, all thought of talk knocked out of them, and slept as they had not done in years. But they had dug the grave nonetheless.

And only when the body was lowered, gently and slowly, did the singing begin. Not one of the psalms that the monks had brought, but an old song, strange and eerie and sad so it broke the heart; a song that had been given from mother to daughter over and over again. It had its roots in a time when there was no time, when there were no books and nothing was written down, when songs and stories were only carried and treasured and remembered.

It was the people of the island who sang it, not the monks. But Neil felt the power of it in the very marrow of his bone, and the song would not leave him all the rest of that day and into the night. As they turned away from the moor at last, the wind and the rain mocking them, he was sure he saw two ravens playing in the sky above until they were swallowed.

But Colum had not come with them. No, he had gone back to his cell and closed the door and put aside his stick. He had gone down on his knees beside the bed and wept until his eyes were empty. And when his eyes were empty and he could cry no more, he asked for forgiveness for what he never should have done.

*

And it was Neil himself who brought Fian back in the end. Larach went with him, almost as much for company as anything else. He was stronger, but still a shadow of the man he had been, and above all else it was his courage that was weakened. In secret Colum muttered that was no bad thing: Larach might live a little longer.

It was the first channel of water that was the worst. They were good navigators both, and Neil probably thought he could have steered between the islands with one hand behind his back, but the storm had driven itself mad and now the wind seemed to come from everywhere. It was all they could do to hear one another, and for a time it felt as if they would go nowhere at all but be driven about instead at the island's edge, fighting simply to keep afloat.

Then quite suddenly they broke free and the prow cut like a knife through the darkness of the waves. They shouted to each other and there was a moment's grin on Neil's face, but it came too soon. They seemed to fight the whole way south, and by the time they turned at last to navigate a whole broken cluster of islets and points of land, Larach was exhausted. It was no less than Neil had feared; he had not wanted him to come to begin with, afraid it would all be too much for him, that his confidence would be diminished the more. Larach crouched in the bottom of the boat, his face white and sore.

'Rest all you need!' Neil shouted as the wind eased. 'This will be different!'

And he was right. The great long south coast of the island beyond was sheltered. The full force of the storm was coming from the north and west, and now they had turned out of its anger. It was a sea in turmoil; the waves dipped and rose, and sometimes a grey cliff of rain drove against them. But still, it was nothing to what they had passed, and Larach himself saw that Neil had meant what he said. He did not sleep, but he crouched in the bottom of the boat a long time, until he felt strong enough to stand once more. Almost at the very moment he did, a watery, misted sunlight broke from the clouds and they looked at each other, smiled and laughed.

'Colum will be praying for us even now!' Neil cried. 'Can you not see him?'

Larach nodded, still smiling. Yes, Colum would be on his knees for them, asking for their safe passage. He thought of the last days of his return from the north and still the tears came to burn his eyes. It was almost too much to believe that he had survived, yet it had happened just the same.

From then on it was not the wind but the sea. Sudden currents that turned them and took them by surprise, and it was the length of that coast Neil had forgotten. It was beautiful, with sudden caves and cliffs and hollowed-out passages, but he had no more than time for a second's glance at such things. All he cared about was that they went fast enough. Colum had been as anxious as they had ever seen him, and it was more than his struggle against illness and age. That they saw and knew well enough, but this was more. And as Neil had not quite understood what went on in his mind that day of the funeral and the burial on the moor, so he could not completely see now. There was something beyond him; something he could not find. A missing piece.

They passed an islet of seals and Neil turned to shout the news to Larach. But he stopped. Larach had fallen asleep after all, was curled in the bottom of the boat.

*

They did not think that even Colum had come so far that he could calm a storm with his prayers, yet what did they know? For when they gathered Fian from Goloch and brought him, slow and careful, down into the boat, still wrapped in blankets, it was all but night. Was it better to wait, sleep a few hours, and start back at first light? Larach was tempted; he fought his own weakness all the time, yet they could not forget Ruach and how he had begged

127

them to return right away. Any longer and it might be too late. Goloch came down to the boat and made sure that Fian was safe where he lay. The boy crouched there, the great bewilderment of orange-red curls flowing over his neck. He spoke to Fian even though he could not hope to hear him, Larach and Neil looking at each other, smiling softly.

'Thank you for all you have done,' Larach said as the boy stood tall, and he clasped his shoulder. 'There is no doubt you have saved his life.'

Neil heard the words and thought at once how Colum would have corrected them. It was not Goloch's doing, but God's alone! You got used to thinking of your answers when you had been with Colum long enough.

'Send me word of how he is!' Goloch called as he started back up the hill. The two men promised they would and then glanced back at each other, the unspoken question in their eyes.

'It's calmer,' Neil said. 'Without a doubt the wind has eased. And look out to the west; the skies are clearer. I think we have to take our chance.'

So it was decided. The whole journey in reverse, and it was Larach that kept watch over Fian and made sure he drank. Goloch had given them precious fresh water, enough and more for the journey back.

And it *was* calmer, almost the calm *after* the storm. Stars above their heads and only sometimes – less and less often – a great boom

of wind. Neil saw a light on the edge of the long coast and he had
the chance to look at it now; he wondered who lived there, for he
had not known there were any folk at all hidden in the shadows of
those cliffs.

It must have been the very middle of the night when they got back.
Lights on the shore then; lights that watched for them and waited.
Neil smiled to himself: it would be Ruach, who else but Ruach. He
would not have rested had he not seen Fian's return with his own
eyes! And there, sure enough, Ruach; moving about and restless
and muttering things to himself. But he was not alone. Colum had
come to wait, too, had made his slow and painful way down the
long path to know that Fian was safe. There was a sadness in his
eyes, Neil thought, and something else he could not read. Yes,
something else.

*

But it was neither Colum nor Ruach who took charge of Fian
that night; it was Baan, the mother of Mara. She had gone to see
Colum herself to ask him, her voice small and quiet, and he had
seen her courage in asking. It would be good for her, and he did
not say no – he could not. In his heart of hearts he had hoped she
would ask.

So Fian was carried in the middle of the night by Neil and Larach
to the door of the fisherman's dwelling. It was wind-still now and
perhaps there would be frost by the morning. Their feet made not
a sound as they bore Fian up from the boat. Only Ruach came
stumbling and chattering after them, anxious and excited. For the

storm inside him had broken; the shadow had at last manifested itself and he was free. He was just a mother hen fretting over her chick now, wanting to make sure that Fian had everything he might need to get better. But Baan would not waste any time on him; she thudded the door shut on Ruach in the end and set to work.

Her husband slept. Huge and dark, his shadow curled away to the wall. She touched him to make sure he slept, and then went back to see to Fian. All that day she had prepared things, though her most precious vials for healing were all but empty. She must not think about that now; she must close her heart to all of it and begin her work to bring him back. There would be no replacing the liquid in those vials before Beltane had passed, but she would give the last drops to him if he needed them all the same.

And so Baan did not sleep at all that night. Instead she banked the peat on the fire so that the flames sprang up from the sleeping embers. She unwound Fian from all the blankets and washed him first, slowly and softly so she did not waken him. Since the time that Ruach had come to him in dream there had been no fever, but he was somehow very far away. His body was weak; she could see the physical evidence of that, and see, too, that his spirit was hidden away somewhere deep inside. There was little she could do but sing, and that was what she did. A song that she had inherited from her own grandmother that was said to have come from the seals. It was the strangest and the most beautiful song she knew, and there were no words. Only sounds to be sung and a story that might be guessed. But to Baan it was a song of healing, that was all she felt for sure. And she sang it now as she washed Fian and wrapped him in new blankets. She rocked him as she might have rocked a young child, for there was healing even in that. And she watched him until the first light came beautiful across the island. Only then did she sleep herself, but not deeply lest he should waken.

Up in the tower, Ruach looked at page after page of Fian's work. He had not been able to sleep and it had not mattered at all. There was a child's joy in his heart that nothing could diminish. Fian had come back at last. He did not doubt that he would be well in the end, though neither did he know how long it might take. But Ruach did not fear that now. Like a young child he turned over page after page, marvelling. The first light broke over the far island and filled the tower. He only wished that Fian might be here now, that they could stand together and talk and laugh again. They would walk down together to the south end and search for green stones. Ruach was anxious for nothing; for once, his spirit was untroubled, and he only wished that his dearest friend might be with him. He was a puppy without its master.

*

Someone was writing in the sand. Fian could see the man, but only from behind. It was as if he was up above him, on a rock ledge perhaps, and looking down. The man knelt in the sand, and the only sound Fian could hear was that of his finger moving as it made letters in the sand. It must have been wet for there to have been any sound at all. Fian did all in his power to stretch forward to see what letters the man wrote, but he could not. He felt maddened for he wanted to know, he had to know – but there was nothing that he could do. He could not go any further forward; it was impossible. But the letters and the words that were being shaped in the sand concerned him all the same, of that he was certain. They were words of life or death, but he did not know which.

*

'What will you do when Fian wakens?'

Ruach was driving Colum almost to distraction. He began to wish that some other dream might take him off to his hidey-hole at the south end, for he was like a little boy who asks why the sky is blue or the moon yellow and will accept no answer until sleep has finally knocked him out. Colum wanted peace to think about many things, and Ruach was not about to give him any.

'I will welcome him back and I will give thanks that he has lived!'

'What will you tell him? Will you tell him or will you wait?'

Colum had been searching for his stick and was furious that he could not find it. Now he stopped and turned on Ruach and drew himself up to his old height. 'I am thinking more what I will tell you in a moment! I wish that you would go and round up a flock of sheep, Ruach! I love you, but not quite as much as I should!'

He found his stick and sighed, and leaned his great hand on Ruach's shoulder. 'I am only glad that he is alive and is here with us again. Is that not enough for now?'

Ruach was left in the shadows. He thought about the words and weighed them like stones in his hands. But the answer only gave him another question, and he was on the verge of chasing after Colum to ask it. For a second he stood outside himself and heard his own racing heart and tongue. He was better off on his own. He would tire himself out walking to the south-west corner and chatter to himself as he went. He was a nuisance and better off out of their way.

But Colum did not forget what Ruach had asked just the same. He would like to have done, but the words of the question echoed in his head all that day, and was there, too, when the last candle flame hissed into silence. What was he to say to Fian but the truth, and how would Fian ever forgive him?

*

And so the spring came, or rather it was born slowly as a lamb might be. There was a day the children went in a flock towards the sheltered glen at the island's heart, and there they found flowers they had never seen before. Yet the next they played and laughed among snowflakes, and for a morning the rocks of the highest hill were white. Larach went, reluctant and slow, to find Colum one evening, and he looked everywhere but Colum's eyes as he spoke to him. He was asking to go to Ireland, for he was restless. And Colum smiled and nodded, not because he was glad but because he had seen and known before Larach came to tell him. What more was there he could do than give his blessing? Yet that night Colum wept, for he had not wanted him to go.

He felt the cold. The wind found ways into his cell and kept him awake. He thought of many things, but more and more of the last

133

journey. He had spoken so often of having no fear, of putting the trembling hand into that of the great hand, yet the wind found him and kept him awake. There were many things he did not understand, and he was not ready. But no one ever was.

And Fian slept. Baan kept watch over him, even when her husband went to the fishing grounds and was gone long days. She watched over Fian. She did not think that he would die now, but she feared many other things. There were times she asked herself why she did this, especially on the nights when the wind came round the dwelling like wolves and the sleet drove against the walls, hour after long hour. Why was it that she looked after Fian? She had only once gone to seek him out and that was to warn him to stay clear and be careful. What was it that she wanted now? What was it that slept in her heart?

A whale beached itself on the west side of the island and it was seen as nothing less than a gift from God in the hungriest time of the year. They left behind only the white frame of the bones, knocked about in the great waves of the high tide, and soon even that would return to the sea.

Sometimes Ruach came to see Fian, though he was afraid of Baan and did not know what to say to her. He would hover outside the dwelling, his hands chasing each other like butterflies, until at last she appeared for more water from the well or to see if there was a drying wind, and there was Ruach, for all the world like a forlorn child. She brought him in, always, and in the end he would even take a cup of milk from her and remember to thank her as she scurried about her tasks and he sat by Fian. He whispered a prayer for him, reaching out to touch his hand, and then he would be gone. Baan came back to find nothing but the cup, and she smiled and shook her head. They were strange creatures, these monks, but they had goodness all the same.

Then at last her husband returned from the fishing and he had torn his cheek. Now she had two sick men to attend to, though Fian was the easier of them by far. It was all she could do to persuade the other to let her sew the flap of skin that first night, and he grumbled and thumped around the dwelling afterwards as though she had tried to stab him. But she knew just the same that he had much to carry. There was a pile of rocks in his heart. She took the mending she was doing and sat on her stool beside Fian, and decided to let the story of the torn cheek come in its own time. It was nothing more than another evening. Still the snow lay on the higher hills, but here on the island the flowers that the monks called Easter lilies were rising again from the ground, and soon their orange-gold trumpets would blow once more in the wind. That was what she was thinking, especially that, when she put down her work for a moment, was about to get up, and found she was looking right into Fian's open eyes. They held her, strong and well.

'Where is Mara?' he asked.

*

Ruach was down at the south end, but not at the beach where he found his beloved green stones. It was a full moon and he was restless, as he always was on such nights. There was no sleep in him; he was wide awake and had to move. He found himself in the jumble of outcrops and cliffs at the very south-eastern tip of the island, as much because he had not been there before. He found a gully that was protected on all sides by smooth walls of stone. Below was a long tongue of golden sand, and at different levels tiny beaches of pebbles. He had to find a way down. He paced the ledge like a caged animal, and then saw what might be half-steps carved by nature at the very end of the gully. He went there and was scrambling down in the blink of an eye. He stepped down and back, and he found himself in a kind of cocoon. For a moment he stopped and looked all about him, unafraid and at peace. He turned to face the sea, looked out of the little gully with its dark rock walls, and there was the whole silver ball of the moon above, not yet high in the sky. Ruach staggered forwards, forgetting in that moment the little beaches and the green treasures they might hide. It was beautiful; he wished he was not alone, that he could have shared this with someone else. Fian would have understood, he decided. Fian would have loved this too.

He went right down to where the tide's edge was lipping the sand. He might have walked out on that silver path all the way across the sea. He felt a deep sadness fill him at that moment, not because of what he did not know but rather what he did. He felt helpless and of no use. There were times when he could be a messenger; he could carry word of things so people understood. That was worthwhile, for all the pain it gave him. But there was nothing to be done with this sadness, for it had not been hidden. He felt the pain of it like the blade of a rusty, blunt knife. Deeper and deeper it cut, with a raw soreness that was beyond description.

In the end the moon passed behind a thin veil of cloud and there was a murmur of breeze – not even as much as that: just a breath. Ruach shivered and for a moment he felt afraid; he looked all around at the walls of the gully as though someone must be standing there watching him. But there was no one. Carrying the broken fragments of himself, Ruach staggered back to the beach he had come from. He curled under the overhanging rocks like a frightened child.

*

'Mara is dead,' Baan said. 'She fell ill after you left. By the time you were carried back she was dead and we had buried her.'

'Dead?' Fian repeated, and was not able to believe the word. He tried to sit up but there was no strength in his arm and he fell back. He thought of the chapel in the rocks where he had gone in the days of storm; he saw himself there again as the one candle flame fluttered above his head, as he prayed and prayed that she might get well, that she might not die. He had prayed as never before in his life, for he was not a monk – he was not one of them. He was a scribe, an artist; he did not have their faith. His was as small and frail as that single candle flame, fighting to endure the storm. But he had believed; he had dared to believe she would be well, that his prayers might be answered. Before he had fallen into fever he had dared to believe it might be so. He did not even feel grief at that moment; he felt nothing but disbelief. It was not possible that Mara was dead. He did not believe it could be.

His eyes came back and he saw Baan in front of him. He did not see her as a mother who had lost her daughter. His head was still slow; he felt so weak. Yet he forced himself to think all the same; to think and to remember. And the morning on the beach came back to him; when she held him and he had promised. He struggled up even though he felt sick and dizzy, for now he had to know. He leaned out close to her and rested himself on one arm. He gathered his words.

'I was sent away. I was sent to the island, after you talked to me and made me promise. For no reason. Colum sent me and I could not say goodbye.'

'It was I,' she whispered. 'I asked him to send you away and he agreed.'

Fian hid his face in his hands and words twisted out of him that were made of darkness. She recoiled from him and he went on, words he had never uttered before that were out of a dead place, a place that smelled. His voice rose and he reached out to drag her from where she sat. She screamed and fell backwards and he was sick. He kept speaking darkness and was sick again. He still saw her and her eyes searched him, appalled, but they could not look away. Until he had nothing more in him and he slid away unconscious.

*

She fed him and he ate. He ate with one purpose only: to leave there and never look upon her again. He had been betrayed. He had been sent away because she had not trusted him, and she had got Colum to do it for her. He did not know for whom he had the greater anger: he hated them both. He had not seen Mara again because of them; they had taken her away from him. What he felt for God he did not know; all he thought of were the hours of prayer in the rock chapel, often as he crouched there shivering with cold as the storm went wild outside. He had been betrayed; that was all he knew.

Sometimes Baan came and crouched close to him (though not within his reach) and asked for his forgiveness. He looked at her with black, hollow eyes and did not blink, until in the end she went away. He heard her crying sometimes, through the night, and he felt nothing; he stared into the darkness and was empty. There came a time when she did not try to talk to him any more, and he rejoiced that she had given up.

One late afternoon he knew he was ready and he got to his feet. The world went dizzy about him but he waited until it passed and then took a step. She was there at once, begging him and trying to block his way, saying things on top of each other until he lunged at her and she shrieked. He went out into the light and the brightness hurt his eyes; water poured down his cheeks and he could barely see at all. He knew that she was behind him in the doorway and he heard her crying, but there was no way on earth he would look back. She must have stood there in the entrance to the dwelling as he staggered away. His heart hammered with the exertion and he felt sick, but he fought his way on. Her voice began to diminish and he knew that she couldn't be following him and he was glad. He stopped when he could go no further and sank to the ground. He felt so sick but he knew he had to keep moving.

He would not even let his eye fall on the settlement or the tower. He walked onto the moors and staggered about there, often walking in half-circles. He stopped many times to rest on stones; he went slowly, trying to find his way dry-shod across the boggy ground. The spring had come even though he barely noticed it. Little fragments of birds fluttered from tussock to tussock and sent out strings of sound. He heard them but he was determined only to get across and to find his way. He thought once that he heard his name called, a long way off, but he did not turn round and never knew if the voice was real or imagined. Night was falling when finally he got there and all but collapsed on the soaking ground. He had promised himself he would drink, from the Well of the North Wind.

*

If he had thought that Mara would come to him, that somehow her spirit might linger in that place she had loved so much, he was wrong. What he felt was hunger and cold. There was no light here on this side of the island; no light on any of the islands to the west. It was cold when the wind came and he kept crouching further and further in to himself, like an animal preparing to hide the winter away. But he would die here; they would find him like this. He imagined that finding and it was the only thing that gave him pleasure.

But he did not sleep. There were times he imagined things, yet he did not believe they were really dreams. He met Colum on the stairs that led up to the book, and Colum could not look at him. He crumpled on the stairs and his staff fell, and Fian simply stood there and the silence was huge between them. Then, about first light, he heard crying somewhere close and he thought then that it was Mara and his heart leapt. He looked all about him and was wide awake, but then he heard the crying again and knew it as the unearthly voices of seals down on the rocks of the west. Their crying was like human crying and he realized it was not night any more; the skies were low and grey. For a moment he felt a fool: he had come here without blankets and without fire, had no refuge of any kind. Before the morning had risen red and gold he had made something for himself; the shelter a beast might have had.

He imagined Baan running to the settlement and to Colum, telling him the news and begging him to do something. She wept and would not be consoled. He would die here and they would find him.

'I have brought you two things,' said a voice behind him, and he spun round in absolute terror, so far away was he in the world of his thoughts. 'Fire and food, and I will share them with you!'

'Ruach!' he cried, and he forgot everything to get up and lay his cheek against the side of the other man's face. He felt the tears sharp in his eyes. Ruach was glad and mischievous; boyish and delighted. There was no shadow in him; no dreams that darkened his day. He brought out the best green stone he had found; long as his hand it was and almost oval, of the deepest jade green. He had polished it until it shone; his pride and his joy.

'I found it one morning at the lowest of tides. There was a beach that normally is not there, at the very corner of the south-east.

141

There was no sea and not a breath of wind, and I saw it from a long way away, prayed that I would reach it before a wave came in. And I did; I found it in time!'

He had brought fire and wood. Yes, everyone knew where Fian was; Baan had come to tell them he had gone and that he would most likely be here. This had been Mara's favourite place.

'What did they say?' asked Fian, when he had refused to have any oatcake.

Ruach looked at him with big blue eyes, as the flames took and grew. 'Colum said: *He is drinking a cup of poison in the hope that someone else will die.*'

A breath of wind came, and still the blue eyes looked at Fian, and then he looked away at last into the fire. The words echoed and echoed in Fian's head.

'She will not come back to you,' Ruach said, and he reached out and held his hand. Still Fian looked into the fire where he crouched, but he could not push Ruach's hand away. He would not look at him, but he could not push him away.

*

It was that day Larach returned from Ireland. He was himself again, the face strong and full, his great hands alive once more. He had been at the monastery of Clonmacnoise and it had been so mild and warm that spring already he had swum in the great curving

142

river that lay below the chapels. It had been a good winter; perhaps in the end the grief had left him and he was forgetting. Colum welcomed him as he might his own son; Larach could see the love in his eyes and it almost made him shy. But he was heart-glad to see Colum just the same; he had feared it might have been his last winter.

'There is one thing I want you to do for me,' said Colum, and he drew him to one side and whispered to him in the shadows.

It had been a fine spring day. The first larks sang in a still sky, and the light was clear over the water. Neil said to the scribes that they were free to go as long as they went swimming. They raced down to the beach where Fian and Mara had sat that last time, and they played and laughed naked in the sea until they could bear the cold no longer. It was as though they were washing away a long winter, Cuan thought. It was not easy to bear the days when there was all but no light and the wind howled relentlessly.

Fian went down from the well to the rough shores on the island's north-west coast. He still carried the last words that Ruach had spoken. He missed Mara, yet did he keep her alive in his mind because he had loved her so much or because he was bitter they had taken her away from him? He felt as strange and lost as ever before in his life; he did not know where to go or what to do. He gathered fragments of wood on the shore for the remains of the fire he had left behind. What would he have done if she had lived, if he had come back and she had recovered? What then? Would it have been possible, or was all that little more than a dream? He knew nothing, or almost. He did know that he had loved her and that he missed her now, that he grieved for her loss and because he had not been allowed to say goodbye.

But his death would not bring her back. All he could hope for was that he might be with her again in the kingdom. And if he was still full of anger for those who had betrayed him, what of his anger for God? Why had he taken Mara away as he did? Was he a jester who played with all the creatures he created?

*

Fian had not eaten for days and he felt strangely good. He drank and drank; the dark cool of the well water reached the very depths of his being. It was as though his senses were somehow heightened, or perhaps it was that he had grown used to silence. He heard the cuff of the wind when it came and passed over the emptiness of the heather and stone; he heard the ravens' squabble as they flew over each other in the blue sky, and he even heard the black rustling of their wings. He was glad that he was where he was and not in the clamour of the settlement. Even in their worship there was so much noise; he had come to the edge of himself and he was clear and ready.

He thought of Mara and went over every word they had spoken together; he dug into the ground that had been theirs and held everything again. He wished that they had had more time. He had come with hatred for Colum and for Baan but he had gone beyond hatred. He did not want to think of them but his dreams were not places where he found his revenge. His head felt empty; he walked and stopped to watch a butterfly in the grasses. He

144

crouched beside a single flower and studied the fur of a bee that hummed against it.

He did not know what remained. That was the question he asked himself; what remained of all he had carried and been through? He knew that he could not have written or painted; he felt that there was nothing left in his hands. He did not even mourn that loss; it was as though the man who had gone up to the tower to his inks had been another.

He was far past hunger and yet there was nothing of him but a thin rack of bones. He went down to the sea one morning and stood there naked, his ankles in the shallows, and he saw his rippled reflection. He somehow had not imagined this was what he had become, and he stared at himself as at a stranger. He stayed awake through most of that night and he felt neither tiredness nor fear. He thought of Ruach, and it flashed through him that he was growing like him. And that pleased him; he was only glad.

*

Did he imagine the secret beach that Larach took him to? Was it part of the delirious wanderings of his mind or did it happen? Was it the following day or the same one? Somehow only parts of that time remained, the way it can be in a dream. He was walking behind Larach and they were going down and down somewhere steep; he was afraid of falling because of the great boulders around them and the deep chasms that lay between. Yet he walked without falling all the same, Larach a few feet ahead of him. They came down to somewhere he had not known before; there was a great dark promontory to his left and a beach of boulders where now they stood. Larach turned and motioned to him, and the sun was in Larach's face; Fian remembered thinking that he looked younger and full of light.

They went to the promontory and Fian saw a kind of jagged gap at the bottom, a low cave that disappeared into the rock. Larach vanished into it and all Fian could do was follow. It was soft under his knees, soft and wet – and he realized that it was sand. He did not like the tunnel; he wanted to be out of it but he could only go on and he fought forward through the dark and suddenly broke out in sunlight. The brightness was fierce in his eyes and he was on a beach, a beach made of sheer white sand. It was shielded on all sides by arms of rock like the one he had passed through; as he looked round, still on his knees, he realized he had come in the only way there was. And he thought to himself that it was a kind of door. But Larach was taking off his clothes to swim; he was saying something to Fian he could not properly hear, but he got up and began doing the same. It seemed all he could do. He followed Larach into the water and it hurt more than anything he had ever known; it was so cold it made him dizzy and the world seemed to tremble. He gasped and was under and he swam, in the blue-green shallows of that secret place. And even then, in whatever state he was, he wished that he and Mara had found this, might have known it together.

And he felt that something washed away. Like an old skin, a whole layer of himself. He thought of the beach where he had started, and the letters and the drawings in the sand. He went under and came up gasping sky, great lungfuls of blue sky. And Larach was laughing, not laughing at him but with him, and he found he was laughing too. He could not remember when he had last laughed and it was good; he did not want to stop.

Then they were not in the water at all but up on the little beach among the rocks. There was a fire made of heather roots that spat and thumped as the flames devoured them, and Larach was turning little fish in the smoke, for Fian caught the scent of them and it was as good as anything he had known in all his life. For a time they ate, hungrily, and there was no need to say a word.

And then it did not seem day at all but evening or the beginning of night, and he was cold and Larach put something around his shoulders. They crept close to the fire and it was red, and he stretched his hands over the heat. And it was as though at last he heard Larach clearly, as though before he had been far off and everything was muffled. Now he heard every word clear and whole.

'I wanted to tell you the end of my story, of my journey back from the north. Because you were not there to hear it; I don't know where you were.'

And Fian remembered; for a second his head dizzied as he remembered that night when he had slipped away. The last time he had seen Mara; the night she anointed his hands.

'I had been with Cormac on a tiny rock of an island: it was he and I who were left. There was nothing, nothing but dark rocks. I remember thinking of the temptation in the wilderness, of turning stones into bread. Cormac went searching for anything; he was beside himself with hunger. He started climbing a rockface because he believed there might be something to find above us. He was mad with hunger. I watched him from below and kept calling for him to come back. He had all but reached the top where there was an overhang of rock. He clawed his way out to the end of it, and then he lost his grip and fell backwards so that his head broke on the rocks. I ran to him and I saw the moment that his eyes emptied and his life flowed away.

'All I could do was to push out the boat and get in myself, weak as I was. I thought of those others who say they are going wherever God would. They have given up their own strength because they have nothing left, and they are carried at the mercy of the waves. That was all I could do.

'I had neither food nor water in the boat and I had given myself to God; I knew that I would die there. I felt no strength left; I had gone beyond myself. And then, Fian, I knew that someone else was with me in the boat. I was in the stern, unable even to rise, and I could see him in the prow, working with things and busy. The sun was almost above me, so looking ahead, all I could see was a shadow. And I knew that we were moving south; I felt the wind at my back, rushing, and I thought of the word south, and it seemed the most beautiful word in all the world. I wanted to say thank you, and I could not so much as move my broken lips to do so. I could only mouth the words. And then he was beside me and he gave me a skin of water. I put it to my lips and drank. Never have I tasted water so sweet and pure and good. I closed my eyes until it was done and when I put the skin down he was gone.

'And ahead of me, Fian – a long, long way off – I saw the island, this island, our island. I knew that I had made it, that I was almost home.'

*

When he awoke, he did not know if he had slept for an hour or a day. He lay curled in close to the well, and the wind played about him in the grass as though it spoke to him. It said that winter was over and spring had begun. He got up and all that had taken place with Larach came back to him, and already it was like a dream. If it had happened, how had he got back to his shelter in the rocks? He had no recollection of returning. He only knew that he felt more himself than ever before. It was as though he had carried heavy rocks when he came here, and now he had put them down. He felt new as the island felt new, and he knelt down a long time to drink from the well.

It was when he stood up once more and moved up onto higher ground above his shelter that he heard the tang of the bell. The first time it was so faint he was not sure if he had imagined it. The wind came again, a soft paw of it, and he heard nothing for a moment. He held his breath and his eyes circled. Then again – the slow tang, tang, that he knew so well. It was still early in the morning and he listened again, as though somehow the sound would tell him more.

So he found himself walking back, not hurrying, over a moorland that was coming alive. The white heads of the cotton grass; the little heads of flowers the name of which he did not know. *Mara should be here*, he thought – but when the words came to him they did so with happiness and he saw her there bending to search for things and telling him the names he did not know. He smiled and she was gone. Now he had walked high enough to be able to look down on the east side of the island and the settlement. He saw figures everywhere and heard the bell's clear call. It lay below the surface of his understanding and yet somehow he felt he knew. Perhaps it was a little like Ruach seeing things without knowing their names. And the sunlight came, full and gold, and spilled over all the ground below like a blessing.

He came down at last among them and they were carrying brooches and carved wood, gifts most precious. He walked among them but they did not notice him; they had come here for someone else. His name whispered a thousand times, with love and reverence and kindness: *Colum*. And so in a single flowing they gathered in the chapel and beyond it, to remember him and the fragments of his memory that were theirs and no one else's.

And Fian saw that none of them was crying. They sang and their eyes were full of light and love, but they did not cry. They came to thank but not to weep. And all at once Fian remembered the day he first arrived, when he had gone timorous to meet this master, not knowing what to expect, and Colum had taken his hands in his to look at them. His would be the fourth pair to work on the book. He smiled now at the thought of it, and at the long journey of the years, and suddenly he felt a fussing with his own right hand. He turned and it was Ruach, putting his own small, girl-like hand in his. And their eyes met a moment. How would Ruach be now, without the earthly father who had been his world? Yet he sang too, broken and hopeless as he was, yet stronger in the strangest way than any of them. Perhaps it was as Colum himself said, that it was broken vessels that let in the best light.

And Fian remembered the anger that had been in his own heart; he remembered it because it was nothing but a memory. It was like an island of darkness one passes on the sea and leaves behind. It had gone. He had come back in time to say farewell; he had not come too late.

*

Afterwards they remembered. The day Colum washed their feet. The day of the storm when he went out himself to meet the boat. The day of the coming of the white horse . . .

Fian slipped away on soft feet from the circle. He had been on the edge anyway and in the shadows; had it not always been that way? He came outside and it was starlight, and as he looked towards the north he saw green flickerings in the sky. Did the heavens themselves know that Colum had died?

For once he did not know where to go. Because he had nowhere, he found himself going down to the sea behind the chapel. He came to the place where he had drawn for the children in the sand, but the tide was high and so he crouched there, on the grassy bank above. He would remember the Colum he had known. Already they were spinning him into legend, and from their stories would be lost the anger and the laughter and the wrong. He had said himself that he was a man who stumbled after God. They would give him golden feet. Fian thought of the time he swept a refectory table of its dishes, of the anger he had for a man who had overslept. And he remembered how he himself had been falsely sent away.

But he knew just the same that he had loved Colum, and that his one regret was that he had never told him. He had loved him despite everything. All at once, gently, he felt a hand on his back. He thought it would be Ruach or Neil or Cuan, and he was glad they had chosen to seek him out.

'Would you come with me?'

He turned round and it was Baan. For one moment they looked at each other, frozen and silent. Then Fian answered as he rose to his feet and held her gaze. Trembling, she reached out her hand to him and it was open.

She took him up onto the moorland, to the place where Mara was buried. He still saw the scar where the spades had cut, but it was healing.

'I wanted to find orchids,' Baan said. 'They were her favourite and they are ready now.'

Together they picked them in the coming night and as he stood with her a dam broke within him and he cried at last. He cried without shame, remembering and missing. They cried together and carried back armfuls of white orchids to mark her grave. And he saw it: this was a whiteness that was stronger than all the dark. The night would not put it out.

When they were done they came down to the settlement and he thanked her, his voice low and shy. She stretched up her hand and touched his cheek. She did not speak and yet it was as though he heard her say: *There will be no more between us.*

He was alone and he knew it was well into the night but there was no tiredness in him. He looked at his hands and he felt things in them; he felt their restlessness. And he smiled. He had made a promise to Mara that he would draw something for her. And the promise was still to be kept.